I0760473

Southern Souls

A MAX PORTER PARANORMAL MYSTERY

Stuart Jaffe

SOUTHERN SOULS

Cover art by Francesca Resta

ISBN 13: 978-1-963517-05-7

First Edition: November, 2019
First Hardcover Edition: February, 2024

For Leann Rettell
she knows why

Also by Stuart Jaffe

Max Porter Paranormal Mysteries

Southern Bound
Southern Charm
Southern Belle
Southern Gothic
Southern Haunts
Southern Curses
Southern Rites
Southern Craft
Southern Spirit
Southern Flames
Southern Fury
Southern Souls
Southern Blood
Southern Graves
Southern Dead
Southern Hexes
Southern Hart

Nathan K Thrillers

Immortal Killers
Killing Machine
The Cardinal
Yukon Massacre
The First Battle
Immortal Darkness
A Spy for Eternity
Prisoner
Desert Takedown
Lone Star Standoff
The Puppeteer
Blowback
Prime

The Ridnight Mysteries

The Water Blade
The Waters of Taladoro
Waterfire

The Parallel Society

The Infinity Caverns
Book on the Isle
Rift Angel
Lost Time
Pages of Glass
The Bold Warrior
City of Infinity

The Malja Chronicles

The Way of the Black Beast
The Way of the Sword and Gun
The Way of the Brother Gods
The Way of the Blade
The Way of the Power
The Way of the Soul

Gillian Boone novels

A Glimpse of Her Soul
Pathway to Spirit

Stand Alone Novels

After The Crash
Real Magic
Founders

Short Story Collection

10 Bits of My Brain
10 More Bits of My Brain
The Bluesman
The Marshall Drummond Case Files: Cabinet 1
The Marshall Drummond Case Files: Cabinet 2
The Marshall Drummond Case Files: Cabinet 3

Non-Fiction

How to Write Magical Words: A Writer's Companion
For more information, please visit ***www.stuartjaffe.com***

Southern Souls

Chapter 1

MAX PORTER LEANED BACK from his desk and rested his head against the wall of his work area — an alcove of the family kitchen. Rubbing his face, he gazed at his laptop screen. He tried to force the words to make sense, but no matter how many times he dealt with the North Carolina government website, it never got easier.

"Any luck?" Sandra said as she walked in.

"You'd think they'd make it simple to give them money. I swear if this is how hard it is to pay our quarterly taxes, I wouldn't dare think about evading them. Way too complicated."

She winked. "Maybe that's the idea."

He watched her body move as she pulled down two wine glasses and dug out a half-empty bottle of merlot from the fridge. Her strong curves, her graceful moves, her sweet aroma — all these years together and she still thrilled him.

"What are you grinning about?" she asked.

"The boys asleep?"

With a short giggle, Sandra poured the wine. "Easy there. Nothing's going to happen tonight."

"Nothing?" He gave her a look that usually worked between them.

"Don't get your hopes up. Not tonight. Maybe tomorrow while the boys are at school."

Max raised his glass. "To tomorrow, then."

She laughed as they clinked wineglasses. "I know it's been a bit of an adjustment with everything that's changed — having the Sandwich Boys under our roof, living in a smaller house, one with thinner walls. It's all been crazy."

"Been kind of nice actually." Particularly having everybody

under one roof. Ever since he and Sandra had moved to Winston-Salem, their lives had been in constant flux. Meeting Marshall Drummond, the ghost of a 1940s detective, kicked off years of strange and dangerous cases involving witchcraft, the dead, and various groups vying for control of those who use magic in the area. But after the recent war between the Mobley coven and the Magi, after Cecily Hull set them against each other and stepped into the vacuum afterwards, after she gave the witch Madame Ti the position of controlling the remaining covens, after all of it, life finally had begun to settle down.

Max and Sandra had lost their big house and much of their good income, but they had the boys now. PB and J lived under their roof, and soon they would legally be the boys' guardians. Admittedly, the roof was rather small, but it sufficed. The neighborhood consisted mostly of starter homes which consisted mostly of starter families — young, ambitious people looking to get a good first step in their lives. Max and Sandra were the old fogies of the block.

"There's that grin again," Sandra said.

"I was just thinking how wonderful it feels to have us all together here. This is our little home, our little family. It's starting to feel like a family, I think. Close to it."

"Give it time. The boys have been through a lot of changes. Not just from living on the street to here, but a lot in between, too."

"I guess it's a good thing my mother still homeschools PB. Let's him have some consistency."

Sandra took a large gulp of her wine. "Don't you dare repeat this, but I think it'd be good for her to come over here. Have dinner with us all. That kind of thing. This whole game she's playing, refusing to see the new house and all, it's not going to end well for her — and that'll make it difficult on us all. I mean, does she really think we'll sell the house and move back into her cramped apartment? Why would she even want that?"

"She doesn't. She just got comfortable being at the center of everything."

"You mean making herself the center."

"It's all an adjustment. Nothing more."

A single-bulb, ceiling-mounted dome provided the only light in the kitchen, and it flickered from loose wiring. Max had intended to get that fixed for the last few days, but they also noticed that if the toilet handle was not jiggled after use, the water would continuously run for hours. He intended to fix that, too. There were other minor issues with the small house, none of which amounted to anything crucial, but added up, they became a thumping headache. One that they needed a good payday to cover.

"We could use a vacation," Sandra said.

"What?" Max coughed his wine, and some of it sprinkled on his shirt — red dots staining the yellow fabric. "Oh come on, this is one of my favorite shirts."

"I'm serious. We should all go to the beach. A real family thing. Besides, in all the years we've lived here, we've never gone to the beach. This is North Carolina — they've got great beaches. Why haven't we gone?"

"I'm not really a sand and surf kind of guy."

"Don't be like that. This is for the boys. They've never even seen a beach."

"How would you know that?" Max sat straighter. "You've already talked to them about this. I'm being ambushed, aren't I?"

Flashing a smile that usually worked on him, she said, "I may have done some preliminary research on the subject to gain an optimal outcome."

Max couldn't hold back a laugh. She shushed him, not wanting to wake the boys, and that only spurred on a heartier noise. Once he regained his composure, he said, "I like the idea of us all going somewhere as a family bonding sort of thing, but the beach — it's too North Carolina hot right now. Do we really want to drive four hours in a car with barely any air conditioning, trudge across burning sand through thick, humid air, all just to lie out under a blistering sun?"

"Yup. We really do."

"You know we shouldn't be spending a lot of money. We're

slowly rebuilding our finances, but business has been rough with most of the witches keeping low profiles right now. Heck, even the hauntings have slowed down. There haven't been a lot of cases coming our way. I guess even ghosts don't want to move around much in hundred-degree weather."

The deep voice of Marshall Drummond said, "You got that right." The ghost lowered through the ceiling and settled near the side door exit. He tipped back his Fedora and thrust his hands in the pockets of his trench coat. "Just because we feel dead cold all the time doesn't mean us ghosts don't sense the weather."

Chiming in, the rattling air conditioning unit kicked off. It never provided much in the way of cold air, but it was better than nothing. Its sudden stop to the flowing air brought the heat back right away.

Sandra finished her wine and took the glass to the sink. "I don't understand you two. I would think all men loved going to the beach. Where else can you see a bunch of scantily clad women showing off their bodies for your pleasure without having to throw dollar bills at a stage?"

Before Max or Drummond could close their gaping mouths, let alone answer, somebody knocked at the door. Strange for anybody to be calling on them, but at such a late hour, it got Max's blood pumping. He reached under his desk and pulled out the 9mm he kept stashed there. He did not particularly like guns, and he still had a lot of training to do before he would wield a loaded weapon, but in his line of work, being armed — even with an unloaded handgun — had become a practical matter.

Drummond stuck his head through the wall. "It's the police."

Exchanging a worried look with Sandra, Max holstered his weapon and opened the door. "Good evening, Officer. There a problem?"

"Good evening, Mr. Porter. I'm Office Glader." The uniformed man had the fit, young appearance of a new recruit. "Sorry to bother you at this hour, but there's a matter that requires your attention."

"What matter?"

"If you'll please come with me."

"What's this about?"

Glader's tone tightened. "Don't make this difficult. If you'll just come along, we'll take care of things quickly."

Drummond floated behind the officer. "He's got a real cop car sitting on the street and he looks like the real deal, but this smells like bad fish, if you ask me."

Max nodded. "Officer Glader, I'll be happy to cooperate. Just give me a moment to call the police department to make sure you are who you say are. Can't be too careful nowadays."

Glader's face blanched. Only for a second, but it was enough to make Max wonder if he could reach his handgun in time. Then he remembered the thing wasn't even loaded.

Glancing to the side, Glader said, "Okay, Mr. Porter. You got me. I am an officer of the law, but this is not official police business. I was told to get you and bring you to a crime scene."

"A crime scene? Why isn't this official?"

"Police don't know about it yet. Officially."

Sandra stepped up behind Max. "Look, he's not going anywhere with you unless you get some specifics out."

Glader rested his hand on his weapon. "Ma'am —"

Max said, "Drummond, please show this officer what he's dealing with."

The ghost swiped his pale hand across the officer's back. Max saw the icy chill register on the man's face.

"W-What was that?" Glader said.

"Who sent you here, and what's this about?"

"Um, well, look I'm just trying to get a few extra bucks, that's all. Honest. I was told about this stuff, you people and the crackpot nonsense you deal with, but what the heck was that?"

"Not so crackpot."

"Don't voodoo me into a zombie or anything, okay? I'm just running a few errands for my employer."

Crap. "Your *employer?* You work for Cecily Hull?"

"Yes, sir. And I've been told that you're needed at a crime scene before the police officially find out about it. That won't last long if somebody stumbles upon it, so please, come with me. If you know anything about the Hull family, you'll know I don't want to screw this up."

"You should have led with that." Gesturing toward the car, Max added, "Just a warning here — don't try anything stupid. That little touch of cold you felt is coming along with us and it can get a lot worse if you threaten me."

Drummond snickered. "You got that right, pal."

Chapter 2

MAX WANTED TO FOLLOW THE OFFICER'S CRUISER, but Glader insisted they go together in his official vehicle. Despite Drummond's protesting, Max did as asked. He figured Glader would not have gone to all this trouble if he intended murder. Neither would Hull, for that matter.

They drove through the city, right by The Porter Agency's Trade Street office, further north, and after a few turns, ended up heading west on 27th Street toward the grounds used for the Dixie Classic Fair — one of the largest and most well-known state fairs. Max always thought of it as the birthplace of every deep-fried nightmare a mind could conjure. Twinkies, bubble gum, Oreos — all deep fried and served up to clog arteries and destroy hearts.

Right before they reached the fairgrounds, Glader turned up Shorefair Drive and pulled into a parking lot on the right. The lot stood empty except for one dented car in the back corner.

"Welcome to Odd Fellows Cemetery," Glader said.

Drummond appeared next to the car. "Sandra's going to be thrilled she missed out on this. There are so many ghosts clogged up here, I can barely see the trees."

Glader kept the engine running but stopped the cruiser so that the headlights did not quite reach the dented car at the end of the lot. "You go on and take a look. That's what she wants."

"You aren't coming?" Max said.

"I've already seen it. And Ms. Hull ain't paying me enough to mess with that car again."

"This is your first job for her, isn't it?"

"So what?"

Max opened the car door. "You sit right there. You may

want to think about finding a different sideline job. This — this is tame compared to whatever else Hull has planned for you."

Glader paled, swallowed hard, and kept his focus straight ahead.

Max stepped onto the carefully lined pavement. Streetlights illuminated the parking lot showing well-groomed trees and well-maintained grass. Stepping in front of the police cruiser's headlights, Max's shadow stretched out towards the dented car. The heat from the cruiser's engine mixed with the humid evening air, and in an instant, the back of Max's shirt dampened.

He walked across the empty lot. In only a few steps, his heart began to pound. The outside of the dented car had been painted with numerous symbols — odd-shaped swirls with jagged lines bisecting them, circles around foreign letters, and even a few religious symbols that Max recognized. White paint had been used and if Max had come upon this car in the daytime, if it had been parked on any street or in any lot with other cars, he would have assumed it belonged to an eccentric, perhaps mentally ill, individual. But out here — Max's stomach turned.

He pulled out his phone and took several pictures. Sandra would be able to identify the kinds of spells these were meant for. And if she couldn't, she would know where to go for the answers.

"What do you think?" Max asked.

Drummond slipped up next to him. "I think doing anything for the Hulls only leads to trouble. But when have you ever listened to me?"

"What was I supposed to do? Get arrested?"

"Might've been a better choice than being out here. Let's get this over with."

Moving closer to the car, Max discovered that the windows were all dark — not tinted but painted black. From the inside. He walked around the car once, continuing to take photos, forcing himself to breathe slowly.

Looking up, he caught Drummond wincing. "What's wrong

with you?"

"I told you — there are so many ghosts here. It kind of hurts to look at."

Max gazed across the area as if he could magically see them. "They all around me now? I don't feel anything."

"They're at the edge of the cemetery. I don't think they have the guts to step out into the parking lot or any further. I suspect they're all tethered there."

"That would mean they're all cursed."

Drummond turned his back to the cemetery. "Yeah. That's exactly what it would mean. After all, Odd Fellows Cemetery started sometime around 1911. Two African-American groups — Twin City Lodge and the Winston Star Lodge — they created this place. And it's one of the oldest and largest African-American cemeteries from the twentieth century. They estimate something like ten thousand graves are in here. And when you look at internment dates, most of the dead are from the Civil War — so we're talking about slaves and others who never lived a wonderful life. That's curse enough in itself. Not hard to believe they are tethered here."

Max stared at his ghost partner with as much surprise as if the dead detective had just risen to life. "How the heck do you know all that?"

"I'm a detective. I know my job."

Max turned in a slow circle. About halfway, he stopped and pointed to the blue sign near the road. "That's a sign from the Historic Society, isn't it? That's got all the information you just told me, right?"

"Big deal. You should be proud that I've finally done some research."

Max stopped himself from throwing out another sarcastic comment. Instead, he smiled. "I am. Good job. You going to be okay to keep working with me here? All those ghosts — are they going to bother you?"

"I'll be fine as long as I don't look directly at them. Gives me a headache, though."

From the police cruiser, Officer Glader said, "Come on.

Quit stalling."

Max headed over to the passenger-side door of the dented car. He gripped the handle but paused. He wondered if a soldier navigating across a minefield felt the same way — knowing something terrible might occur in the next breath. Or maybe it would all be fine — just another false alarm. Bracing himself for whatever sights and smells he might encounter, he opened the door.

The rancid smell of bowels and blood wafted out. Max reared back and covered his mouth. His eyes watered. Pausing long enough to keep from doubling over and throwing up, he tentatively breathed in again. After giving the car a moment to air, he crouched forward.

A middle-aged man sat in the driver's seat. He wore a black raincoat that had been painted with many of the same symbols found on the outside of the car. His head angled back as if snapped hard. Bits of his skull and brains painted the back seat. A shotgun rested between his legs with the muzzle pointing upward. One hand lay on the steering wheel and the other at his side as if he might drive off for an old time cruising.

Max had seen dead bodies before, and he had seen more than his share of the ghosts associated with those bodies, but rarely did he come across such a blood-soaked mess. "You see this guy's ghost anywhere?" he asked Drummond.

"If he's here, he's off in the cemetery. I'm really the only ghost in the parking lot at the moment."

"I don't get it. He's not around here and those symbols are wards — but you're still here. You don't seem affected by anything. What's so special about this guy that makes Cecily Hull drag me out with a police escort?"

"Check the glove compartment. That's always a good place to look."

Max pulled down on the glove compartment latch. Sifting through the papers, he found the car registration and insurance. The name listed — Wilson Klein.

"At least, we've got this."

Drummond flicked the brim of his hat. "See? I've watched

you do wonders with only half a name. You've got the whole thing this time. You go on your computer and spend a few hours researching, I'm sure you'll find plenty on this guy."

"Glad you have such confidence in me, but that doesn't answer why Cecily Hull wanted us out here. Officer Glader could easily have found out this guy's name by running the plates or checking the glove compartment. Hull could have simply given me that name and asked me to research the man. But she wanted me out here. There's something we haven't seen yet."

"You mean other than the ridiculous number of symbols painted all over the car and his raincoat? He even blacked the windows so he could paint more symbols on top of that."

Max forced himself to stare at the body longer. Something itched at him. Something seemed off. When it hit him, he marveled that Drummond hadn't seen it first. "This guy supposedly committed suicide — but look at his hands."

Drummond leaned forward, his body slipping through the side of the car. "Well, take a gander at that. If he had killed himself, his hands would've flopped to his sides. Somebody positioned him afterwards."

Max glanced back at Officer Glader. "You think it was him?"

Staying focused on Wilson Klein, Drummond said, "Not a chance. That cop is so green and scared that if we don't get out of here soon, he might wet his precious cop car."

Max snapped a few pictures of the body's position. He had read that forensic photographers grew numb to the experience of photographing the dead. They could be photographing bowls of fruit or pretty vistas — it all became the same. But Max's skinned prickled as he clicked several more shots. He thought about the old tribal beliefs that pictures captured part of a person's soul. Knowing what he did about the world of ghosts, he found himself wondering what he should consider true.

"I can't be sure," Drummond said squinting at Klein's hands, "but I swear this fella's pointing at something."

Max looked closer at the hand on the steering wheel. The index finger did appear to be pointing forward and at a slight angle. He stared into the dark copse of trees and licked his lips. "You really think he's pointing out there? I mean, there are all kinds of explanations why his finger ended up that way. Perhaps he —"

"You can sit here coming up with excuses all night long, but we both know where this is going to end. Might as well get moving out there now."

Max's head snapped toward Drummond. "You're not coming?"

"Listen, partner, I've always got your back. But I can barely look into those woods. I won't be any use to you. I won't be able to look around, won't be able to help search for evidence, nothing. But I'm still here. If you run into any serious trouble, then you start screaming. I'll go in there anyway. I'll do what I can to help."

Max looked back at the dark tree line like a small animal stirring at the mouth of a cave, wondering if a bear slept inside. "Fine. But if I die —"

"Yeah, yeah. You'll haunt me forever."

Max backed away from the car. "This man here was moved after he died. I'm not misinterpreting this, right? It means he was murdered. "

With a solemn nod, Drummond said, "Be careful."

Swallowing down the rise in his throat, Max headed toward the tree line. When he entered the wooded area, the temperature dropped. Even in the nighttime, this area remained cooler. No. Ghosts riddled the cemetery grounds. With their spectral bodies as condensed as Drummond had indicated, Max recognized the cold chill that continued to strike his skin. He waded through ghosts.

Up ahead and to his left, the land opened up for the graves. With so many Civil War-era African-Americans buried here, a large number must have been slaves. Most of their graves would be unmarked. But to his right, Max glimpsed a flicker of firelight. Trying not to let his mind wander or wonder, he focused on that light. Even as he marveled, he continually moved forward. The near constant icy chills from walking through ghosts threatened to send him running out of the woods.

Several feet in, he found a small altar that had been set up against two trees twisting around each other. The altar consisted of an old wooden stool covered with a moth-eaten cloth. Two candlesticks covered in old wax sat on the stool. One had the liquid remains of a long red candle. The other bore a black candle which still flickered its light. Two old photographs leaned against each of the candlesticks.

Max paused to scan the woods. He did not want to meet whoever lit these candles. Stepping closer, the air around him warmed. Apparently, the ghosts did not like this place and left it vacant.

He picked up the photos. The first depicted an old, wood slat house — barely more than a shack — black and white photo, something from the early 1900s. The second photo prickled Max's skin as if touched by one of the ghosts. Also black and white, the photograph was of six white coffins. They were laid out on black tables, saw horses, and gurneys. A crowd of men stood solemn and cold with their hats clutched low — their dress again suggested early 1900s. The coffins varied in sizes, including two distinctly small ones.

Officer Glader honked the horn of his cruiser. Though Max did not jump, his heart certainly fluttered through several beats. He swiped the photographs, shoved them in his pocket, and hastened toward the parking lot. The more distance he put between him and the altar, the better he felt. Dealing with a police officer out of his depth seemed the better choice than hanging around a candlelit altar in the woods.

As Max neared the cruiser, Officer Glader stuck his head out the window. "I just heard on the radio — somebody called this in. Police will be here soon. It's time to leave."

Max glanced at Drummond. The old ghost nodded. "Either somebody waited to call this in for a reason or —"

Max tried to keep his voice calm. "Somebody might be

watching us."

Glader said, "All the more reason to get your ass in my car. Besides, you're not done yet."

"There's more?"

"Cecily Hull wants to talk with you."

Feeling a wobble in his legs, Max hurried into the police car. "How about you take me to jail? That might be more pleasant."

"Sorry. I'm not officially here." As Glader drove away, Max made sure not to look in any of the mirrors. He did not want to see those woods ever again.

Chapter 3

OFFICER GLADER HEADED SOUTH, straight into the center of Winston-Salem. With midnight approaching, the roads were fairly empty, but even those loitering on the streets kept to themselves. After all, nobody wanted to bother a police cruiser at night.

He turned onto West 3rd Street and parked next to Merschel Plaza — a grassy park on two levels. The bottom level was open land which could be used for a variety of purposes. A narrow walkway covered a strip on top about the width of the street. People could walk along this path, picnic, or simply use it to cross into the buildings toward the south. Cars had parking underneath. Just west of the Plaza stood an apartment building — the bottom floors in brick and the top floors painted off-white.

Drummond floated outside the car. He stared at a large grassy lot to the east of the Plaza strip. "That used to be the Pepper Building. Gone now."

Max did not like the troubled look on the ghost's face, but whatever the man's past with the Pepper Building, it would have to wait for another day. To Officer Glader, Max said, "Where am I supposed to go?"

Glader nodded his head toward the apartment building. "Somebody'll be in the lobby. Take you to the top floor."

"Of course they will."

As Max exited the car, Glader put his hand on Max's arm. "Please, tell her I did a good job."

"I will. But you promise me you'll go find some other job. Or stick to being a good cop. Jobs like this — they're only going to lead a guy like you into trouble."

The moment Max closed the door, Glader had that cruiser halfway down the street. "Do me a favor," Max said to Drummond. "Go back to the office."

"The office?"

"You can go to my house if you'd like, but you don't seem to care for the Sandwich Boys all that much lately — not since J started getting glimpses of you."

"Now hold on just a second. I don't get bothered by people being able to see me — you don't bother me and neither does Sandra — so don't start blaming your problems with the kids on me."

"I love those boys. I look forward to them really connecting with me, making a real family. You're the one who seems to be trying to put distance between you and them."

Drummond tilted his head and eyed Max carefully. "I'm not sure what's going on in your head right now — I'm fine with those boys. Heck, now that J can see me, I like him better. Maybe we should just focus on this impending interview with Cecily Hull and leave the rest for another day."

Max looked around to make sure nobody had seen him arguing with an empty space on the sidewalk. "That's why I wanted you to go to the office. Or my house or wherever. Cecily Hull is not an idiot, and she has Madame Ti as her number one witch. Do you really think that building is going to let you in? There's got to be ghost wards on every floor, in every window, and every stairwell. I figured you could do without all that pain."

If Drummond's pale skin could have reddened, Max figured he would be as pink as a glass of zinfandel. The old ghost said, "Oh. Right. Then I guess I'll see you in the morning." He did not wait around for a response.

Max headed toward the apartment building with a mixture of amusement and concern battling across his face. His soft steps sounded loud in the quiet night, and he wondered if visiting Cecily Hull alone was any less dangerous than entering a copse of dark woods filled with ten thousand ghosts. With a shudder, he pushed off where those thoughts might lead.

Turned out Officer Glader was wrong. Max never got inside the lobby of the building.

As he approached the front door, a large man wearing an expensive but ill-tailored suit stepped outside — clearly a bodyguard, clearly armed. One look at Max and the man gestured him over.

"Ms. Hull isn't ready to see you just yet," the man said.

Max puffed up his chest and cocked his head to the side. "You can call up and tell Ms. Hull that I've had enough of her toying with my night. Either she can talk with me or I'm going home. I had my fill of these power games back with Mother Hope and the Mobleys. I don't need any more of it from her."

He felt only half as brave as he sounded, but the big man did not have enough information on Max to know that. He raised one finger before turning back and making a quick call on his phone. Seconds later, he returned. His face gave nothing away nor did his voice. "Follow me," he said.

The big man led Max around the side of the building and down a short alley. A metal door painted to match the brick stood flush at the back. The big man pulled out a tiny keyring and opened the door. Gesturing, he said, "Just follow the stairs up."

Feeling like a guy stepping into a hidden speakeasy during the 1920s, Max entered a narrow stairwell and proceeded to climb five flights. However, unless this imaginary 1920s fellow headed toward a meeting with a mob boss connected to witchcraft, the similarity ended there. Max chuckled. Drummond probably knew of real mobsters who had used magic.

But that was the 1920s. In the present, having a secret entrance to an apartment situated in an apartment building seemed silly and redundant. Then again, Max did not have the kinds of enemies a Hull attracted. He paused on the stairs. Actually, he shared many of the same enemies. Maybe he should get a secret entrance to his house and office.

The top of the stairs ended with a concrete landing and a simple metal door. He knocked.

He figured most of this exercise in door knocking and secrecy had been put in place to display the level of power Cecily Hull had attained. But to Max, this amounted to a bit of theater and little more. While she certainly had rebuilt some of her family's former wealth, and she had clearly maneuvered herself back into a position of attaining some power, the disarray of the witch community proved that nobody had become the ruler of magic in North Carolina. Not yet.

The door opened, and a young man with military hair and wireframe glasses bid Max welcome. "Ms. Hull is ready to see you now."

He led Max down a corridor with tan fabric-covered walls and dim lighting. The fabric dampened most sounds and gave the space an artificial aroma. Several dark wood doors on either side remained closed while soft classical music played from well-hidden speakers. At the end of the hall, the young man opened a door on the right and moved aside.

Max stepped straight into Cecily Hull's office. He imagined the door on the far wall led to her actual apartment, but he suspected he would never see that part of the building. Never really wanted to, either.

Cecily Hull's office brought together a strange mixture of styles. Her desk sat in the center of the room — made of glass and metal, no drawers, a simple and elegant and thoroughly modern design. Behind her, a floor to ceiling window looked out upon the Plaza, shedding natural light across the entire room during the daytime. This late at night, the window appeared more like a picturesque mural of city lights.

Yet the modernity changed with a wall of built-in bookcases of dark wood. Dusty, leather bound books — ancient and archaic texts, no doubt — filled the shelves with forgotten lore. It was a private library that most witches would have killed for. Some probably had tried.

Cecily Hull stood behind her desk. Tall and stark, she splayed her skeletal hands on the glass and leaned her head to indicate the uncomfortable looking chair in front of her. Speaking in the exacting, clipped manner Max only associated with her — even the slight Southern tinge to her accent did nothing to soften her tone — she said, "Mr. Porter, have a seat."

Max did not want to sit. Sitting implied that he would be spending more than a couple of minutes in the office. But he did not want to be rude, either — at least, not yet. He sat.

She looked him over and her mouth tightened. "In the future, should you ever come here again, please have the courtesy to wear something clean."

Max glanced down at the wine stain on his yellow shirt. "Perhaps next time you can avoid the threat of police and I won't feel obligated to leave without changing my shirt."

"I apologize if Officer Glader acted overzealous. Thank you for accompanying him this evening."

Max shrugged. "You didn't give me much of a choice."

"I know that you do not like me. I do not expect you to be my friend. I have no need for friends. But the deaths of Grandma Mobley and Mother Hope have had greater repercussions upon the magic-using communities than ever were created when you defeated my Hull relatives."

"If our lack of magic-related cases is any indicator, I think things have been improving."

Cecily tapped her fingernails on the glass before turning toward the window. "What did you think about the suicide at the cemetery?"

Like a bratty teen, Max crossed his arms and leaned his chair on its back two legs. "Sorry, but I don't work for you. You want somebody to do research or look into whoever that was that died, go hire somebody."

"That is exactly why you are here. I wish to hire you for this case. I know you do not want to do this, of course, and I would be lying if I did not say I agreed with you. However, at the moment the world I live in is still in flux. Until I have better control over the situation, until I have my own people in place to do your job for me, I want to hire the Porter Agency to handle this matter. Someday I'll have no need for you, and I am sure you will be delighted when that time comes, but it is not today."

She turned around and did her best to offer a charming smile. Max's skin crawled at the unnatural sight. With a single clap of his hands, he popped to his feet. "No," he said and strode toward the stairwell.

He expected her to protest. He expected the door to be locked. He expected the big bruiser from outside to be standing in his way. Instead, Cecily said, "When you change your mind, call me. But do not wait too long. Wilson Klein is only the beginning of this."

Max wanted to whirl around and offer a snappy reply, but his desire to leave that building overcame his desire to be sarcastic. He hurried down the stairs, and when he reached the bottom, an electronic sensor slid open the door out.

The bruiser was nowhere to be seen. He thought about walking to the Porter Agency office — only a few blocks away — but he did not want to hear Drummond's attitude. The old ghost would simply reiterate what Max had already thought and said — that the Porter Agency wanted nothing to do with Cecily Hull.

He got out his phone and ordered a ride share to take him home.

A half-hour later, Max sat in bed with Sandra curled under his arm. He recounted the entire evening partly to get her up to speed and partly to release all the tensions that had built up over the course of the night. When he finished, she asked to see the pictures he had taken of the dented car.

Max reached for his phone and showed her all the symbols. "You recognize any of it?"

She shook her head. "There are so many ancient languages and private witch languages that nobody could know them all. If you want me to, I can look into it."

Setting his phone back on the nightstand, he said, "This really isn't any of our business. The fact that Cecily Hull wants us to investigate it suggests that it must be connected with some group making a play against her attempts to control all of the witches."

"Then doesn't that make it our problem?"

"Only if we're going to get into the business of deciding who runs things around here. That's the same old game we got caught up in before. It seemed like a good idea the first time around with the Hull family, but that didn't really work out. We got rid of them — for a while — but then the Mobleys and the Magi all thought they should each take over. Somebody's always going to try to grab the power. I think for us, the best we can do is wait until the dust settles and figure out how we fit in."

Sandra kissed his chest before propping up on her arms. "You know what's so strange is the way those symbols were all over the car. I've seen symbols laid out on the ground or on the corners of buildings or any number of other places, but there always seems to be an order to it. This just looks like a madman spewed everything out on his car."

A gentle knock sounded against the door, and PB stepped in. In a meek voice, one Max had never heard out of the young teen's mouth before, PB said, "I think I know about those symbols."

Max and Sandra both bolted up straight. Sandra said, "You know what those symbols mean?"

Max said, "You were eavesdropping on us?"

PB started to turn back but J stepped into the room. Despite being smaller, J crossed his arms and blocked the way. The two boys exchanged a look before PB turned back. With a heavy sigh, he said, "I got something important to tell you."

Chapter 4

MAX SHOULD NOT HAVE BEEN SURPRISED that PB and J heard his discussion with Sandra. This wasn't their old, large house. This was a starter home. There were only a few feet of hallway between the bedroom doors and the walls were thin.

The four gathered together in the living room — the largest space in the house with barely enough square footage to place two couches and a wall-mounted flatscreen. PB and J settled on the blue couch (PB's favorite) while Max and Sandra sat on the brown couch that hid stains well. Sipping from coffee mugs — coffee for Max and Sandra, hot cocoa for the boys — they watched each other with a mixture of love and wariness.

Max wondered if all families felt this way when confronted by something big — at least, something that felt big. He had concern for PB, fear over what the boy might say, and an unsettling shiver that this could be the landmine he always worried about stepping upon. If he and Sandra failed to handle PB's problem, the boy might never trust them again. After all, how could PB and J accept them as parents if they failed their first test?

PB had grown in the last few years — his chest had broadened, his face had become more angular, his muscles more defined. Yet he never lost the cautiousness in his eyes. The boy acted like a war veteran always on the search for the next threat, the next ambush. Max wanted to assure him that they would not be behind such an attack but lacked the words to cut through the boy's defenses. If he and Sandra screwed up this time, PB might never listen to them again.

J, on the other hand, approached life with a gleeful joy that never failed to warm Max. He had spent the same time on the streets as PB, and he was smaller, easier to pick on. As a black male, he suffered plenty of prejudice from people and the systems of society. Yet despite all of that, he never gave up on the world. He let his intelligence shine.

"It's going to be okay," Sandra said. "We're here to listen."

The words sounded hollow to Max's ears. The look on PB's face suggested that he felt the same. J nudged PB with his foot, and PB shoved J back.

"Don't make us wait all night," J said.

"Shut up." PB tried to avert Max's eyes. "I'll get to it when I'm ready."

As soft and kind as Max could pipe into his voice, he said, "Take all the time you need."

At length, PB said, "Only reason I'm bringing this up is that I heard you talking about a bunch of symbols and that they were like a madman threw them all over the place. Y'all have come across strange writing before on your cases, and I never heard you describe it like that. Thing is — that's exactly how I thought about the writing I saw."

Max pulled out his phone and brought up the pictures of the car. "Take a look."

PB swiped through several of the photos and nodded. "That's them."

"Who?" Sandra asked.

"The people who killed my dad." PB lifted his head, and his eyes shimmered. "Same people I think are coming after me."

Max could feel Sandra's tension rising up alongside his own. With a shiver in her voice, she said, "What makes you think that —"

"I ain't stupid. I know what I saw."

Max put one hand on Sandra's leg and the other out toward the boys. "Let's all calm down and hear what's going on. You tell us whatever you've got to tell us, and we'll do everything we can to help you, to protect you."

J leveled a stern look at PB.

"I said I would," PB said. "Stop given me the eye."

But PB held still, closing his mouth with a subtle shake of

his head.

As if PB had punked out of a dare, J said, "Oh, come on, man. After all this, you going to have to tell them."

A memory flashed in Max's head — floating above his own body at Forsyth Hospital. Mother Hope had cursed him into that strange existence, and at one point, PB snuck into the hospital room while everybody else was away. Thinking Max could not hear him, or perhaps wishing he could, PB tried to tell him a large and terrible secret. The fear on PB's face matched the fear he now held.

"Close your eyes," Max said. "Think about that time at the hospital."

PB's head snapped up. "You heard me then?"

"I guess so. I didn't realize it until now. You trusted me then when I couldn't do anything to help you. Trust me now. Trust us."

Like an older man confessing to a priest, PB hunched his shoulders and kept his eyes upon his fidgeting fingers. "I loved my dad. He took care of me and my mom. Made sure we had a roof over our heads and food on the table. He wasn't always around, but he did his best. My mom — she was high all the time. When my dad was away, I spent most of my days trying to keep her from doing anything stupid."

"Sounds like my childhood," Sandra said.

PB gazed at her for a moment and shared a knowing nod before he lowered his head again. "One night, I don't know why I did this, I guess I was just fed up, but when my dad said he had to go out for a couple hours — and that often meant a couple days — I had to know where he was going. I got it in my head that he had another family. I kept picturing him with a perfect wife and a couple kids who did nothing wrong, and he gave them all his money, and well, I just had to know." PB shuddered. "I kind of wish it had been another family. It would've been easier to take."

Max sipped his coffee, but he had no need for the caffeine boost. PB's intensity electrified the room.

"We lived downtown," PB continued. "So, my dad just

started walking, and I followed. Block after block. He ended up in a part of the city where all the signs are in Spanish, and he met up with a bunch of other people in the yard behind a little, blue house. I didn't get it at the time, but I've had years to think about it — I'm pretty sure all the backyards that met up against that one, that all the people who owned those yards were there that night, too.

"Anyway, I hid behind some bushes and watched. They all took off their clothes and put on these black robes with hoods on them, and they made a big circle. A bunch of those weird symbols were painted on the backs of the robes."

Max looked to Sandra, but she put up a hand to stop him from speaking. A nod in PB's direction reminded him that the boy had enough trouble getting this far in his story. They should let him speak to the end.

"One of these guys wore a purple robe — different from the others. I figured he was the leader. He rambled on for a while about a bunch of crap I didn't care about. I still don't. Stupid sounding names and words and things. But I did get what the point was — money and power. The leader said that soon they were going to have all the money and power they could dream of, and I'll never forget this part — he said they were going to rival Skull and Bones."

"What's that?" J asked.

"I didn't know at the time but I looked it up later." To Max, PB added, "You'd be real happy. I did some serious research."

Max smiled. "I'm sure you did a great job. What did you find out?" No point in ruining PB's moment by showing off that he already knew the answer.

Huffing a little, PB said, "Skull and Bones is this not-so-secret secret society. It's kind of like a fraternity for rich people. They help each other out through their lives with powerful stuff like getting to be Senators and Congressmen and for running businesses. Stuff like that. Probably a bunch of illegal crap, too."

J said, "Woah. And your dad was one of them?"

"Seemed like it. But it also seemed like they were trying to recruit my dad and all those other folks. Because they started asking for tribute — which I found out later was a fancy way of saying give them money. And that's when I started thinking about all the stuff that had been stolen from our house. Stuff I assumed my mom had pawned off for drug money. But then I started thinking that maybe my dad had been pawning it off to get money to give to these whack jobs. Or maybe he just gave them the stuff he stole. I don't know, but it was real crazy to me. When I got older, that's when I started thinking the whole thing wasn't a special secret society, but it was a cult." PB dabbed his palms against his eyes. "I think my dad tried to join a cult."

Max didn't know what to say. As PB had described it, this group did indeed sound like a cult — a bunch of people filled with desperation choosing to give their worldly possessions to a charismatic leader who promised wealth and power at some nebulous point in the future. Max could almost believe it. But those symbols — they were the aspect of this that did not ring true to a blind cult. Those symbols spoke more of a coven or at least a loosely-organized group that explored witchcraft. Of course, that could still operate like a cult. But the world that Max resided in took the witchcraft aspect far more seriously.

Another nudge from J's foot and PB said, "I'm getting there."

"There's more?" Sandra asked.

PB nodded. "They spotted me. At least, I'm pretty sure they did. I shot out of there fast like if the police had shown up. I never felt my heart pound so freaking hard. I didn't stop running until I got home.

"My dad comes back later that night and goes straight to bed. Next few days things between him and me are really tense, but he never mentions any of it. After two days, I started thinking maybe I'd gotten away with it. Maybe they hadn't actually spotted me, and I just got scared."

Max had a dark thought. "But that was wishful thinking, wasn't it? They did spot you."

"My dad disappeared. Not like before, not going away for a

few days. He flat out was gone. Usually he slipped away with some clothes and such. But he left everything behind. Including his wallet with all his cash. My mom and I, well, neither of us reported it. I think I hoped he'd be coming home like normal sooner or later. But in the end, when I was starting to get ready to call the police, they came knocking on my door. They were rude and mean, talking like my dad didn't really matter because we were poor and crappy people, but the cops did make it clear — my dad was dead. Said it was a car accident."

"But you don't believe that."

PB lifted his head and stared straight into Max's eyes with a ruthless, feral glare. "I don't have to believe it one way or the other. I know. Next morning, I walk outside and find all those symbols painted on the sidewalk in front of my house. That's when I thought they looked like a madman threw it all up on the concrete. You get it? They killed my dad. They killed him because I followed him. They killed him because I saw what I wasn't supposed to see. I'm the reason he's dead."

"No. None of this is your fault."

PB launched forward until he stood in the middle of the room, breathing hard and sweating. "I'm the reason they killed him. Me. And now there's another one of them out there killing people again, painting weird symbols everywhere. They're going to come for me soon. You look into that guy who died, and I guarantee you're going to find that he saw something he shouldn't have seen. Just like me. These people — they don't take to the loose ends. That's what I am. I ran away from home so they wouldn't go after my mom. When you found me and started having me work for you, I figured they'd never bother looking for me right under their noses, right here in Winston-Salem. I don't even use my real name. But I can see now that I was stupid. They're coming for me, and I can't stop it."

Sandra rushed over and wrapped her arms around PB. Though he tried to stay tough, stay stoic, in the end her embrace forced him to fall against her chest. He buried his tears against her.

Max stood and pulled out his phone. "Don't you worry. I

won't let anything happen to you." He tapped a number and waited for the ring. When he heard a greeting, Max said, "Cecily Hull, you've just hired the Porter Agency."

Chapter 5

WHEN MAX WOKE, he stayed in bed, stared at the ceiling, and listened to Sandra getting breakfast ready. Running on only four hours of sleep and dealing with the physical crash that followed his caffeine-adrenaline boosts left him with a desire to curl under his covers and blot out the world. Not even a full Thanksgiving dinner could bring on sleep as strongly.

But then he heard PB mumble something and Sandra returned with a sarcastic groan. He heard J bounce into the kitchen with all the exuberance of a puppy ready to play. Eager to set the table and get his day at school started, J jabbered nonstop. No chance Max would be getting back to sleep.

He sat up in bed, rubbed his eyes, and gave his cheek a firm slap. He had a job to do. More importantly, he had a job to do for PB. After a quick shower and half-a-cup of coffee, he settled at the kitchen table with the boys and Sandra. To PB, he said, "I don't want you to be worried about any of this. We're a good team and we know how to find answers."

PB spread his hands out as if placating an idiot. "Why would I be worried? Just because there's a bunch of crazy people in robes out there thinking about killing people — probably me. No reason to worry about that. This'll be a snap."

"I didn't say it would be easy. I'm just saying we've got your back."

"Okay, boys," Sandra said as she started clearing the table. "It's still a school day. Get your stuff together."

"I have to go to school today?" PB said.

"Absolutely. Grandma Porter is expecting you."

Max still winced inside whenever he heard his mother referred to as *Grandma Porter*. They had tried out a few other names — Gammie, Granny, Meemaw— but nothing quite fit. Max even suggested Professor Porter since she was PB's main homeschooling teacher. But despite the witchy images the name *Grandma Porter* inspired for Max, everybody else had grown accustomed to the moniker.

"I just thought," PB went on, "that with it being dangerous right now, I shouldn't be following my normal routines. Isn't that what you suggest to your clients when somebody is after them?"

Max said, "Right now, it's more important that you're someplace we know is safe. My mother will take good care of you, and if anything were to happen, she can contact us right away. But nothing's going to happen. We don't even know if anybody is actually after you."

"We don't know that they're not after me, either."

Sandra rattled the dishes in the sink before turning around and placing one hand on her hip — never a good sign. "Number one, you're going to school. Number two, if these people really wanted you dead, they had many years to take care of it. Don't go around thinking you're some superspy that kept yourself below their radar all this time. And number three, *you're going to school.* Now clean up and get ready."

PB and J knew enough to hurry out of the kitchen. Once they were in the bathroom brushing their teeth, Sandra turned to Max. In a softer tone, she said, "Am I telling the truth? Was he right? Do you think somebody's actually after him?"

Max downed the last of his coffee. "Anything's possible right now. We need to do our research today. Find out what we can. Then we'll know whether to be worried or not."

"That wasn't very reassuring."

"You wanted me to lie?"

"A little judicious truth-stretching would be appreciated."

"Oh, in that case, of course we know he's fine. After all, we've got those symbols. Anybody practicing some form of witchcraft, no matter how strange, would have known how to cast a location spell on PB. Since that's never been done, I'd say he's fine."

Sandra leaned over and kissed the top of Max's head. "I love you."

"Sheesh. If I knew it was going to be that easy to get you to love me, I'd have lied to you a long time ago."

She giggled. "So, where do we begin?"

While in his morning fog, Max had been thinking about their research strategy. Now that his latest dose of caffeine had kicked in, he tapped on his phone. "I'm sending you the pics of those symbols. I'd like you to look into them, see what you can find out."

"Already expected you to give me that job. I've got a few ideas of where to find what we need," Sandra said. "You going to be at the office?"

"I better. If I stay here, chances are I'll end up in bed asleep."

Sandra grinned. Over her shoulder, she called out, "Boys, time to go."

Max sat back with a grin of his own. "You're starting to sound like a real mother."

"See that? Maybe we're not so bad at this after all."

Drummond lowered through the ceiling. "Doll, you could never be bad at anything."

Moping as he walked, PB crossed through the kitchen, out the side door, and headed toward the car. Sandra turned to call for J once more, but he bounded in, slinging his backpack across his shoulder, ready to face the day's academic challenges. His joyous gait stumbled as he looked up at the ceiling. Though he kept walking, he never stopped looking at Drummond.

"Come on, now," Sandra said, giving J a gentle push on the shoulder. "In the car."

With less bounce in his step, J exited the kitchen. Drummond said, "I thought you two talked to him about me. That he understood and it was all worked out."

"It is. A little." Sandra snatched her keys off a hook by the side of the door. "But now that he's seeing you, I think he's starting to see more and more."

Max said, "I didn't know it could work like that. I only ever see Drummond."

"Some people are like you. Tuned into just one ghost. But a lot of people — especially the young — once they wake up to being able to see, they start to see everything. We can talk about it later. I've got to go."

Sandra dashed out. After she left, Drummond floated to the floor.

"I'm going to be doing research all day," Max said. "You're welcome to hang out with me, but I know how much you love watching me read books and stare at computer screens."

Drummond snickered. "You don't have to play me in order to get me to do what you want. I know what you're going to ask. You want me to go into the Other and see if I can find Wilson Klein."

"Am I that predictable? Sandra knew exactly what I was going to ask her to do, too."

"I don't know how predictable you are — wait a second, I do. You're very predictable. But in this case, we all have our skills and talents. It makes sense that you would ask us to follow up on the things we're best suited for. But if you want to be a good leader, try to remember that we're more than just those few things. Trust me. It took me a long time to let that one through my thick skull. Save yourself a lot of grief and start learning it now."

Max cocked his head to the side. "You've already been to the Other, haven't you? You've already started looking for Klein."

Drummond removed his hat and gave a little bow. "I have indeed. He's definitely in there. Quite a few of my contacts have seen him around. Word can travel fast in the Other — that place loves gossip. Too many bored ghosts with nothing better to do than flap their jaws. Well, some of them don't have jaws anymore, but they still manage."

"Then Klein probably knows you're looking for him."

"Yeah, but I'll get to him. Don't worry."

"Me? Worry about you? Never."

Resetting his hat, Drummond said, "I've got some good

ghosts helping me out. I'll get him and bring him in."

He disappeared, and for a few seconds, all became still and quiet. Max tempted himself with the idea of crawling back to bed. He lost track of several minutes before snapping awake.

"Better have another cup of coffee," he muttered and juiced up his system with more caffeine.

By the time Max arrived on Trade Street, his head had cleared and his body had fully woken. He climbed the stairs to the small office — enough room to house a desk for him, a desk for Sandra, and the bookcase built into the back wall for Drummond. They had a small bathroom and an area with an old couch and a low table for eating. A large circular rug covered the casting circle Max had carved into the floor for Sandra's practice. Beyond that, the office could have been used for any small business.

Flopping into his chair, he powered up his laptop and got to work. For the moment, he focused on one easy target — Wilson Klein.

Klein's death had already made it onto the local online news sources, and reporters were calling the death a suicide. The articles provided nothing much about Mr. Klein except for the street he lived on — Goldfloss Street. That tidbit of information would make it easier to separate Max's Wilson Klein from all the others in the state of North Carolina.

Next, he searched the Winston-Salem Police Department records. But at the moment, the case had not been closed and therefore not made public. That meant that either the paperwork on the suicide had yet to go through the department bureaucracy or the police were not considering the death a suicide and keeping the case open.

Max turned to spending a little money and used several identity websites meant for employers or landlords to record check potential employees or tenants. Armed with the address from the article, Max waded through the numerous hits until he found the Wilson Klein he wanted. The information proved rather underwhelming.

Wilson Klein, age 34, lived an unremarkable life — single, renting part of a house, working the same entry-level clerical job for the last seven years. No criminal record. Nothing, in fact, that made him standout as special or threw up red flags as troublesome.

Max stared at the screen. "What could a guy like you have done to get yourself murdered?"

He spent the rest of the morning searching through news articles, Facebook feeds, image searches — anything that might clue him in on what aspect of Klein's life made him a target. In the end, Max had found nothing. The man had few friends, did not belong to any clubs, had no serious hobbies, had nothing that would have brought him into contact with a criminal element or anyone dangerous. Especially witches. Other than finding Klein's dead body in a car covered in odd symbols, Max had nothing to connect the man with anything strange or supernatural.

Around noon, Sandra entered the office carrying a cardboard box filled with Chinese take-out. He had no memory of the time passing, but his stomach rumbled at the smell of food. As they ate, he shared the limited and unremarkable information he had discovered. Sandra paid close attention as if what he had to say held great importance.

When he finished, he said, "I don't get it. Are you hearing something different than I'm saying?"

"Not at all." She set her pork lo mein aside. "Here's the weird thing — you're telling me that Wilson Klein has no connection to witchcraft, no connection to anything criminal, no connection to anything. And that is exactly what I found out about those symbols. They're not connected in any way to witchcraft or the occult or anything. Unless those symbols are from a private coven that never let any of its members write down a single word that could be found later in history, then the only thing I can say is those symbols are made up. They're not real."

Max set his food down with a thump and paced back and

forth in the eating area. At length, he plunked down on the old beaten couch. He felt like an innocent man waiting to hear if a jury would wrongfully convict him. Not that Max faced such a serious kind of trouble — or maybe he did. After all, technically this case belonged to Cecily Hull. For the moment, he worked for her.

"Well, this is just great," he said with a huff. "We've got a murder made to look like a suicide, we've got a victim who has no reason to be murdered, and the whole thing is covered in witchcraft symbols that aren't even real."

"Hey, hey, honey, what's bothering you?" Sandra said. Before he could answer, she raised her hand. "Don't tell me it's this case. Obviously, it's frustrating, but I know you too well. You don't get upset over this kind of thing. If anything, I would expect the lack of information to be an exciting challenge. You'd normally be back at your computer doing more research before I could finish eating. You should be fired up. So, what's the problem?"

Max closed his eyes. He wanted to say that Cecily Hull's involvement had knocked him off balance, but the words tasted wrong in his mouth. When he did speak, his expression came out slow and thoughtful. "Everything feels disjointed. Not here — but at home."

Sandra chuckled. "Of course it feels disjointed. We moved to a smaller house with a bigger family, less money, and less assurance that were going to be okay. Everything is up in the air. But we've lived in worse situations, or did you forget the year we spent in a trailer?"

"And it was Cecily Hull who got us out of that situation."

"Are you worried that you took this case because you wanted to get out of the situation we're in?"

Max rubbed his chin. "We've always wanted to build a sturdy foundation for our family, for the boys. When it was just the two of us, all the craziness in our life was fine. We held hands and pushed on through it together. But now — now these boys really do belong to us. They really are our responsibility. It's not just a dream or some paperwork that needed to be filed. They live under our roof. Before, they spent time with us, but it was always temporary. It felt more like playing at being parents. Now, it's real. I want us to all come together as a family, yet I don't know if this is what it's supposed to feel like. How do we know when we've actually achieved it?"

Sandra sat on the couch and put her arms around him. "Honey, the fact that you're even asking that question tells me that you're doing just fine."

"I don't know. Maybe my mother was right."

"Don't ever say that again." With a stern look that held an amused twinkle behind the eyes, she went on, "Your mother has been a big help in many ways and a big pain in the ass in many more. I think her self-imposed distance has been good for us. When she's ready — and when I'm ready — we can melt some of that ice. But for now, under our roof, she is never right."

"Okay, okay. She's never right."

Sandra pecked his cheek. "As for our family — you've got to understand that all families are different, and ours has to be very different because of all that we deal with. But it's still family. It's still important." Her eyes widened. "That's what this is about."

Max frowned. "I thought I've been pretty clear."

"We're doing this case for PB's sake, and you are worried we're going to fail him. You didn't find anything about Klein and neither did I, and that's got you freaked out — not because Cecily Hull is paying the bills on this one, but for PB's sake."

He had to admit that her words felt right. "I suppose. That's a good thing, isn't it? I should be worried about how this all plays out regarding PB."

"Of course. But that's your answer right there. You're worried about our family becoming a family and how it's all going to fit together, yet you are acting like a father who cares for his sons and wants the best for them. You are trying to protect one of your boys, and that defines us as a family already."

Max got up and grabbed Sandra's lo mein. Taking a few bites, he said, "I wish I could simply take your words and make them solid in my heart. But until we find out something about Klein that we can use, it's hard to believe that I'm going to protect anybody."

With all the bravado of a conquering warrior, Drummond entered through the wall. "Did I hear you say you needed something on Klein? Your great and ghostly partner has delivered."

Max noticed Drummond's arms were held in a funny way — as if locking somebody in a tight grip. Max looked to Sandra. She nodded. He said, "You did it? You got Klein?"

Drummond tilted his head up. "You had doubts? Max, Sandra, I give you Wilson Klein."

Chapter 6

MAX LEANED AGAINST THE EDGE OF HIS DESK as he watched Drummond struggle with the air in front of him, forcefully guiding the ghost of Klein into Sandra's casting circle. They had all been through this routine before. Max had seen it enough that he could approximate the writing in a pinch. It wasn't too difficult to lockdown a ghost for a short period of time. But Sandra grabbed chalk from her desk, got on her hands and knees, and scrawled several new symbols on the edge of the circle. Ones that Max had never seen.

"I got this idea during the witch war." She explained that during that tumultuous time, Madame Ti had locked a ghost within a casting circle and somehow made the ghost visible.

"But I was under a curse then," Max said. "I thought that's why I could see and hear the ghost."

"It was. But you were only a half-ghost. You shouldn't have been able to see him so clearly. Plus, Madame Ti could interact with the ghost just fine. Which meant that something about her spell made the ghost within the circle visible and audible. More than any spell I've ever encountered."

Wriggling his arms in one direction, then another, Drummond said, "Whatever you're going to do, get on with it. Klein is not too happy about being here, and I can't hold him forever."

As she wrote more symbols, Sandra said, "I can't guarantee this will work in making Klein visible, but it will hold him down. Don't worry about that."

She stood, closed her eyes, and mumbled several words to herself. Then she stepped back. With a nod, Drummond let Klein go and slipped out of the circle. Apparently, Sandra already knew how to select between more than one ghost for capture. Max didn't want to know how difficult that trick was, but he suspected she had been working harder at it than she let on. Since she was determined to become one of the first good witches in existence, Max figured this was probably the right place to start.

A tinny sound rose in volume. As the sound grew louder, a hazy shape formed in the circle. By the time Max could make words out of that sound, he could see Wilson Klein standing in front of him — no more than a fuzzy silhouette but a shape nonetheless.

"That's amazing," he said, peering over at Sandra. "How long have you been working on that?"

"Ever since I saw it. It's not very good, but I think given some more practice I might be able to bring up the full image of a ghost."

Drummond said, "Doll, if Max is seeing anything, what you've done is incredible."

"Then it's incredible," Max said.

Pounding his fists against the air in front of him, Wilson Klein said, "What kind of people are you? You've locked me in a circle and all you do is sit around congratulating each other?"

"Watch it, pal." Drummond drifted to the edge of the circle. "You do not want me to come in there."

Sandra stepped over to Max. "That spell won't last very long. You better get on with it."

Max took a cleansing breath. He needed to be myopic for the next few minutes. Ghosts, witchcraft, PB, family — all of it had to be shut out. Only one thing could remain. Wilson Klein.

"Mr. Klein," Max said, lowering his voice. "I'm sorry we had to bring you in against your will, but we need the answer to some questions. After that, you'll be free to go."

Klein's shadowy form shook his head. "You all are morons. Absolute idiots."

"Why were you at Odd Fellows Cemetery?"

"Seemed like a good place to die. Made it easy to get my body in the grave."

"You didn't kill yourself. We know you were murdered."

"I'll murder you, if you don't let me out of here."

Max tapped his chin as he thought. Clearly, Klein would continue to be belligerent until they grew tired of asking questions. But nobody could be happy about having been murdered. Perhaps some brutal honesty would do the trick.

To Sandra and Drummond, Max said, "You know, I think Klein is right. We're being fools. There is no way this man was killed for some special reason."

"Oh, gee, no," Klein said in a mocking sing-song. "Now you're going to try some kind of pathetic attempt to get in my mind." He raised a closed hand, and the distinct silhouette of his middle finger lifted from his fist.

"Not at all," Max said. "I'm just realizing that we're wasting our time talking here. I've already looked into your life. There's not much there."

Drummond said, "Hold on. I went through a lot to get him here."

"Sorry about that, partner. But while you were off trying to find him, I spent the day looking into his life. Fact is that Wilson Klein had no life. Nothing really significant. He was basically a bland, boring loser."

With his shadowy hands clasped to his shadowy head, Klein said, "Loser? You are terrible at your job if that is what you think. I was selected by the greatest man to ever live. He chose me."

"Who chose you? Chose you for what?"

"If we are all to prosper, then we must all be willing to do our part. The great Soro Brown knows this. He has true gifts, true power, and through him we will all become great."

Drummond reached into the circle and grabbed Klein by the shoulder. "I've had enough of your crap." He punched Klein. Just once, then let the man go.

Sandra said, "Stop that. Beating him up is not going to get him to cooperate."

"Maybe not, but it made me feel better."

She walked around to the other side of the circle and knelt

near Klein. She pulled out her phone. "I completely understand why you don't want to talk with us. You've been assaulted, kidnapped, forced into this casting circle. Not a very welcoming way to get you to answer questions. We're not really mean people, but in this case there's somebody very close to us, very important, who might be getting caught up in whatever you're involved with. We're trying to protect that person."

Rubbing his chin, Klein said, "I don't care."

"We're talking about a young boy." She brought up a photo of PB. "This boy. All we need from you is some basic information. We'll do our best to make sure you don't have to betray anybody, but if you'll —"

Klein pressed up against the invisible barrier of the casting circle. "That's amazing. Soro Brown was right." He pushed back and skipped around the circle. Shouting — nearly singing — he said, "Soro Brown was right. He predicted and it is all coming true."

Scratching the back of his neck, Max watched Klein parade around the circle and tried to come up with an alternate approach. Direct interrogation had failed. Good cop/bad cop had not worked. And appealing to morality floundered. Max did not hold out much hope. Getting a straight answer from Dracula's old pal, Renfield, would probably have been easier.

Max lifted his head, about to say something sarcastic to simply relieve his tension, when he saw Klein's shadowy figure flicker. "Um, I think the spell is wearing off."

"Don't worry," Drummond said. "I can just —"

Klein disappeared completely. In the next second, Drummond's head popped back. His hat flew off, disappeared, and reappeared on his head as the old ghost fell through the wall. Max moved to get in front of Sandra, but a cold blast raked his chest. Klein's frozen hands grabbed the back of Max's head and slammed him downward. Max's training in martial arts had taught him how to control his fall. If not for that, his head would have bashed into his desk — possibly killing him. Instead, he rolled his body and clipped his shoulder against the edge of the desk.

As he struggled to his feet, Sandra screamed, buckling to the ground. Drummond soared back in, both fists clenched and ready. Hovering in the middle of the room he spun in a circle.

"He's gone," Drummond said.

Max helped Sandra to her feet, and the two huddled on the edge of the couch.

"You want me to go after him?" Drummond said. "I will. But I don't think he can help our case any. Still, I wouldn't mind returning a few punches."

"No," Max said. "Pissing off that ghost is only going to muddle things up. And frankly, we don't want to be having that ghost screwing with us right now."

"Does that mean you have a plan for what to do next?"

"Not a clue."

They stayed quiet for a minute. Straightening, Sandra said, "We need to talk to somebody who has a chance of knowing what this is all about. Somebody who knows why fake symbols would be used or why this fake suicide was set up."

"Or who Soro Brown is," Drummond said.

"Exactly."

"You got somebody in mind?"

She looked to Max and then Drummond. Max could feel her bracing herself for his objections. But he needed to be open-minded, thoughtful, and appreciative of any idea a member of his team brought forth. And that went double for his wife.

Sandra said, "I think we should see Madame Yan."

Max threw up his hands. "Oh, sure. Let's get a witch involved."

Chapter 7

MADAME YAN LIVED ON THE EDGE OF LEXINGTON near Speedy's BBQ. The few times Max and Sandra had come to this witch's home, the delicious smell of Lexington pulled pork BBQ drifting through the air reminded him that even in the most wonderful places, the dark side of the supernatural existed. Granted, Madame Yan did not treat her witchy powers as a right to abuse others — at least, Max had yet to see that side of her. No matter what though, the woman was a witch.

At the moment, however, he had to deal with another woman who had shown her darker side — his mother. Sitting in his car, he kept his phone on speaker so he didn't smash the thing through his skull. "All I'm asking is for you to pick up J from school. Either Sandra or I will come by tonight to pick up both boys, but our current case is running a little longer today."

"I understand exactly what you're asking of me," Mrs. Porter said, her tone shifting into her parental discipline mode — sharp as a carving knife. "The point is that I am not your personal chauffeur service. Ever since you moved out of my apartment, you've all acted as if I am doing nothing all day but waiting to help you. I'll have you know that I live a full and rich life."

Max pinched the bridge of his nose and closed his eyes. "I'm sure you do, and I truly hope that asking this favor is not impeding any plans you have for this evening."

"Don't get fresh with me."

"I'm not. I only meant —"

"I know what you meant. I'm not some old lady sitting alone at home who couldn't possibly have a social life or anything to do."

"I'm not suggesting —"

"I'll admit that since I moved down here, I've not been as active in my community as I try to be, but that is because I've spent my time helping you get your life back on its feet. It seems now that you are doing fine. I'm happy for you. Truly I am."

"Thank you. But just because we've moved away, doesn't mean we don't need you to be part of our life."

"And I'm glad to hear that. I wish being part of your life meant more than taking care of your responsibilities. You know, I like being Grandma to the boys. I do. But I have other interests. I like movies, the symphony, the theater — there's no reason why you and I couldn't go do some of those things together."

Max opened his eyes and saw Sandra step out of Madame Yan's faded-yellow rancher. "You're right. When we pick up the boys tonight, we should make some plans to go do something like that. Right now, I need to know that you'll get J because I have to work on this case so that I can make money so that I can feed the boys."

"You know I'm going to pick up J for you. There's no need to get all dramatic about it."

After a few more subtle and not so subtle jabs, Mrs. Porter hung up and Max let out a sigh. Sandra opened the passenger side door and leaned in. "It's all set up. According to her assistant, Cheryl-Lynn, we'll be interrupting Madame Yan's afternoon snack. She's doing us a favor by letting us visit on such short notice. She said that Madame Yan hasn't been feeling well lately — I think Cheryl-Lynn hopes a little witch business might cheer the old woman up. As long as we're okay with all that, then we can go down and see her."

Max got out of the car. "I don't want to see her at all, but we've got to do it. So, let's go."

As he started toward the trailer, Sandra paused and looked back. "You coming?"

Drummond appeared, floating to the side the car. "Not a chance. Witches generally don't like me. I'll wait out here."

Max frowned. "How long have you been there?"

"Don't worry — I didn't hear much of your conversation with your mother. Frankly, I wouldn't want to hear it anyway. Now get in there and get to work."

Walking up the well-maintained lawn, Max refocused on the witch at hand. Because Madame Yan was no ordinary witch. Even amongst the witch community, Madame Yan was considered peculiar.

She lived up a narrow lane in a poor section of town despite having enough money to build a large underground study. Where all the surrounding homes were littered with toys, weeds, or half-built muscle cars, Madame Yan's rancher was well-maintained and bore a simple sign on the door: *Enter and wait.* She went to the expense of having a personal assistant managing her life, but she never appeared to leave her home or do anything that required assistance. Even her assistant was peculiar — a woman who wore a black hijab over a white frock, had smooth, olive skin, and wrinkle-free dark eyes that suggested she was in her early 20s. Yet when she spoke, her strong North Carolinian accent jarred the image she had built up.

Stepping into the cluttered living room — mismatched furniture shoved up against the walls and each other — Max strolled through an arch leading back toward the kitchen. He had been through this routine enough to know where to go.

Still, Cheryl-Lynn insisted on leading the way. "I'd be pickled in brine if I let you wander around this house."

She led them downstairs, through the false basement designed like a medieval dungeon, and down the narrow, hand-carved stairs to the real dwelling beneath. She stopped. Like always, she did not go any further. Apparently, threats involving garlic-soaked salt water did not extend further than the stairs.

Max and Sandra hunched over as they proceeded across the wide, low-ceiling basement. They knew the ceiling would get even lower as they went. At the far end, a single hanging bulb guided their way. They came upon the wooden door that always gave them trouble. After three hard pulls, Max managed to yank the door open enough to slip in.

Madame Yan's underground apartment remained the same overstuffed, chaotic mess as usual. Of course, she had books stacked everywhere. But she also had stacks of newspapers and magazines from bygone eras. She rearranged the room often enough that while the hoarded clutter always remained, the specifics changed. Where once she had a box full of old bottles, now she had a pile of damaged puppets. A tray with empty glass vials perched precariously on a tower of children's alphabet blocks. Two stuffed owls watched from the corners near the ceiling while an iguana — apparently living — clung to the side of an old bookcase.

From the back room — a room Max hoped never to encounter directly — the pleasant aroma of chicken soup floated in. "Just make yourselves comfortable," Madame Yan said, her voice lower and scratchy. "I'll be right out."

Sandra shrugged and moved some moth-eaten coats off a stool. Max opted to stand.

When she entered, Madame Yan held a mug of hot soup. She was heavyset, yet when she moved, she flowed with uncommon grace. Her voice, her face, her very being was an amalgam of cultures and regions throughout the world. This visit, however, her nose was red and her eyes swollen. She sat in her high-backed chair and let the steam of her soup play over her face.

"Ho," she said without her typical verve. "Madame Yan is here."

"I'm so sorry," Sandra said. "We didn't know you were sick."

"Just a little cold. Nothing to be concerned about."

Max said, "I'm surprised you witches don't have a spell to cure a cold."

"If we had that, we would never have been hunted down and persecuted for centuries. The world would have embraced us if we could cure their ills — at least those basic ills."

Sandra pulled out her phone. "Since you're not well, we will be direct and quick. We don't want to make you have to use too much energy. You need to rest."

The old woman chuckled. "You're mothering a witch. Be careful. I might come to like it and not let you leave."

Max's muscles tensed. Despite her vulnerable appearance, a witch was a witch. He knew to never take chances with their little comments.

Sandra explained about the murdered man in the car filled with fake symbols, and she alluded to PB's experiences with the cult that may possibly have killed his father. Madame Yan set her soup aside and picked up Sandra's phone. She swiped through one photo after the other and then handed it back.

"Oh, yes, indeed. I know exactly what that's all about." She picked up her soup and blew on a spoonful.

Crap. Like all witches, Madame Yan would not give her information for free. She sipped her soup and waited.

She reminded Max of a garden gnome — small, hidden amongst the leaves of her books and collections, and ultimately, mischievous. Sandra crossed her legs and watched Madame Yan. Max got the impression that a battle of wills had begun, but seconds later, he revised his thoughts — Sandra would not be foolish enough to play that kind of game with a seasoned witch. She had a different angle in mind.

When Madame Yan finished her soup, she set the empty mug on a wobbling tower of other used soup mugs. "I can see you have thought this through," she said to Sandra. "And since you are still here, I will take that to mean you would like to hear my terms."

"Be careful what you ask for," Sandra said, keeping her expression still and uninformative. "I'm not the newbie you met years ago."

Max's jaw dropped wide open. Sandra's growth in witchcraft had given her some serious guts.

Madame Yan shifted her whole body toward Max. "You better watch this one. You make her mad, she'll turn you into a toad." With a devilish grin, she gazed back at Sandra. "Okay, here it is — in exchange for telling you about those pictures, I request one of your favorite lipsticks."

Sandra's face screwed up as she snorted a laugh. "Lipstick?"

"One of yours."

"Oh. I see."

"Consider it an insurance policy." With a grumble, Madame Yan scooted to her feet and waddled over to a mound of odds and ends. After rummaging around for a moment, she pulled out a box filled with lipsticks. "It's for my collection."

"But also to use in a spell. A spell on me — should the need arise."

"Well, dear, I wouldn't be a witch if I just gave everything away. Now, what's it going to be?"

Max wanted to grab Sandra's hand, yank her to her feet, and pull her out of that house. They had enough already — Madame Yan had admitted that there was more to this story which meant that Max could research. Put in the hard work and he could find the answers. No need for this kind of a bargain.

But even if he pranced around barking like a dog trying to warn its human, he knew Sandra would not pay attention. He could see it in the way she held her shoulders and the way she lifted her chin. She had locked into a battle of will and intelligence, and it was her duty to make sure that she left with the upper-hand.

Without taking her eyes off Madame Yan, Sandra reached into her purse and pulled out her lipstick — an old one Max did not recall her using in years. Did that make a difference for spell casting? Before he could protest, she said, "We don't have the time, hon. PB's counting on us."

With those words, he revised his view of the situation. Sandra was not playing mind games at all. She simply wanted to save her boy. She handed over the lipstick.

Max rubbed his thumb into the side of his head to stave off a headache. Thoughts ping-ponged around his skull, but the answer never changed. Sandra was right. All of this reduced to a simple idea — PB was in trouble, and they were his only chance at fixing things. While Max believed he could come up with answers given enough research time, Sandra understood it better — they didn't have the time. Or maybe they did — they didn't know. But they couldn't take a chance with PB's life.

He rested his hand on Sandra's shoulder and gave her a short squeeze. Her hand came up and clasped his. She leaned her head back against his stomach.

Madame Yan plucked the lipstick away, placed it in her box of lipsticks, and returned the box to the piles of rubbish off to the side. Pulling a stained handkerchief from her pocket, she blew her nose and settled back in her chair. She gave a short cough, and Max wondered if the witch might deliberately try to get them sick with her germs.

"Your boy's father was not in a cult," Madame Yan said. "Rather, he had joined a tragedy group."

"A what?" Max said.

"They probably have other names now, but that was what I always heard them called. A tragedy group. These are people who have no talent for witchcraft or no connection to the energies of the other worlds. But they believe that by controlling the bad energy of the tragic moments of life, they will somehow be rewarded with good in the future. Not a religious deity type of thing, rather more like a karmic idea. Now, this murder suggests the group is one of the darker of such groups. There were a few that gained popularity in North Carolina over the last few decades."

She hopped to her feet again and dug around a stack of books on the other side of the room. Finding the one she wanted, she wiped away at crumbs or dirt — Max did not know which and didn't want to know. Thumbing through the pages, she said, "Let's see. Those symbols suggest — yes, right here." She showed Max and Sandra a page headed with a row of symbols similar to the ones found on the car.

"The Soro Group," Max read.

"Yes, a little play on words. *Soro* and *sorrow*. They use the word as one might use an honorific like King or Reverend or even Madame."

Sandra said, "Then Soro Brown could be anybody with the last name Brown."

"Now according to my book here, the Soro Group believed they needed to spill blood on three tragic sites in order to earn their reward. So, including your dead friend in the car, how many of these have you found?"

"This was the first."

"Then there's your answer. You can expect two more of these." Madame Yan snapped the book shut and tossed it aside without care of where it landed. "I'd say that's enough information for a lipstick. You two are smart enough to figure out whatever else you need. And, while I always enjoy a visit from you, I really need to rest. I feel awful."

Without another word, Madame Yan shuffled off into the back rooms of her underground dwelling. Sandra and Max sat still for a few moments, digesting what they had learned. At length, Sandra stood, and holding Max's hand tight, they worked their way back to the surface.

They moved slowly. Max's thoughts jumbled in his head. As they walked from the kitchen to the front, Cheryl-Lynn opened the door and smiled. "Y'all come on back whenever. We like having you around."

Stumbling toward their car, Max and Sandra moved like zombies as they tried to process what had happened. They settled in and drove off. Drummond must have seen it on their faces because he kept quiet for a full five minutes.

But eventually, he burst. "One of you tell me what the heck went on in there."

Max pulled into the last gas station before hitting the highway. With only a few interruptions from Sandra, he detailed their visit with Madame Yan.

At the end, Drummond said, "Are you out of your mind? You gave her your lipstick?"

Sandra said, "Should I have hung PB out to dry? Would that have been better?"

"That's not the point."

"It absolutely is."

"But you gave her something that belongs to you. Of all people, you should know what that means."

Sandra whipped around. "Of course I know. But I am not going to let anything happen to that boy — even if it means taking a risk with a witch."

Drummond's face pleaded with Max. "You just got out of a witch's curse. Are you really going to let her get caught up in a new one? You want her to go through that?"

Forcing his voice to remain calm, Max said, "This isn't helping. The three of us fighting won't solve anything. The lipstick has already been given away. It's done. I'm fairly certain that Madame Yan won't let us simply take it back. So, if you want to be helpful, let's work the case in front of us. Let's help out PB, so that Sandra's sacrifice was worthwhile."

"But —"

"We solve this case first. Then we can focus our energy on getting Sandra free from whatever Madame Yan might do."

Tapping the headrest with her fingernail, Sandra said, "Don't forget that just because Madame Yan has my lipstick doesn't mean she's going to use it. She had dozens of them in that box."

Drummond shook his head, but he also pursed his lips — a sign of him working through a case. "You may never get that lipstick back. You understand that? If she doesn't use it to cast a spell or a curse, she'll hold it over you for the rest of your life."

"It's a risk I had to take," Sandra said. "But Max is right — we need to focus on PB's case right now. Then, I promise, we can do whatever needs to be done to protect me. If anything can be done."

"Besides," Max said, "of all the witches to give a personal item to, Madame Yan is probably the nicest. We may never have to worry about her actually doing anything with it."

Nobody spoke a word, and the silence filtered out the lie Max wanted them all to believe. "Okay," Drummond finally said. "We now know that Klein's murder was all part of this tragedy group. We also have a name, Soro Brown, to look into."

"That could be anybody," Sandra said. "It's not like Max can get anywhere researching Mr. Brown."

"Then let's go over Wilson Klein's crime scene again." Drummond walked them through each step of their approach to the car and the way it had looked. They all checked over the photos on Max's phone and discussed the way Klein had appeared. Drummond suddenly clapped his hands together. "The finger."

"What finger?" Sandra asked.

"He was pointing into the woods with his finger. Sort of. And Max went in and found a little stool. Right? With some candles. But then we got taken away by Cecily Hull's rent-a-cop."

Max's head spun. How could have been so stupid? He grabbed his coat and rifled through the pockets. "The pictures. There were two photographs in those woods." He pulled them out and held them up for the others to see.

Drummond only glanced at the photos before he drifted backwards. "Damn."

Sandra grabbed the photographs. "A big funeral and an old shack of a house. You know what these are?"

With a bitter nod, Drummond said, "The Lawson farmhouse. And all those coffins are the Lawsons. What you're looking at is one of the most famous, most brutal massacres in North Carolina history."

Chapter 8

AS MAX PULLED ONTO 52 NORTH and headed toward the office, he listened closely to Drummond's story. Sandra faced the back, and Max could tell she tried to console Drummond with her sympathetic expressions. Looking in the rearview mirror, he could see that Drummond's attention had turned inward — into memories of long ago.

"It was 1929," Drummond said. "Actually, it was Christmas — December 25th. Can you believe that? Fellow by the name of Charlie Lawson had bought a farm up in Germanton. It's a town a bit north of Winston-Salem. From the stories I heard, he had a fetching wife and seven well-raised kids."

"Seven?" Sandra said. "I mean I know that was pretty common back then, but still — seven."

"Well, it wasn't so strange to see a large family like that — especially a farmer's family. But not everybody had them like that, either. And so close together. Their eldest was only seventeen, and the rest went down all the way to four months old. Just four months and that bastard killed them all."

"So they caught who slaughtered the family?"

"That part was easy. Charlie Lawson did it. Killed his whole family." Drummond shifted his hat and watched the scenery race by the window. "As I understand it, a little bit before Christmas Charlie took the whole family into town — Winston-Salem — had them buy new clothes and had a family portrait taken. That was pretty strange. Back then, that was an expensive trip. Today, you can drive to Germanton in about fifteen minutes or so, but in the 20s — getting the whole family loaded up, hitching a horse, since they couldn't afford a car, going all the way to Winston-Salem, buying new clothes, having a portrait taken — that was an all-day affair. Lawson spent a lot of money on that."

Max said, "You think he was planning on doing this then. This was premeditated."

"I think so. But who knows. The whole thing is madness."

As he described the events that followed, Max could see it unfold in his mind. It was the afternoon of Christmas. Lawson sent his eldest son, Arthur, into town on some silly errand. Having gotten rid of the only real threat, the man put together his arsenal and waited by the tobacco barn. When his daughters, Carrie and Maybell, came by, he pulled out his twelve-gauge and shot them both. He dragged the bodies into the barn and bludgeoned them to make sure they were dead.

Next he went straight up to his house and shot his wife on the porch. His eldest daughter, Marie, was inside baking a cake. She must have seen what happened — certainly heard it — and she screamed.

A blind rage then took over Lawson. He burst into the house, shot Marie, and then hunted down his two young boys. His raging steps clumping on the old wood floor would have terrified the children. After disposing of them, he murdered the four-month old baby. Bashed the poor thing to pieces.

With his whole family destroyed in a matter of minutes, Charlie Lawson walked out into the woods. As people discovered what had happened, they assumed Charlie to also be a victim. They started searching for his body.

"The story I heard is that when he shot himself, the sound echoed for miles. A little while later, folks finally found him, and there was a well-worn circle where he had been pacing for hours."

"This picture," Sandra said, "These are all their bodies."

Drummond nodded. "I didn't know the Lawsons. Never would've heard of them if not for this sensational story. Read about it in the papers. Everybody was talking about it."

"But one of the children survived."

"Arthur did because he wasn't there. Really messed his head up worse than any shellshock or such could ever do. But other than him, none of them survived."

"But there aren't enough coffins in this photo."

Drummond dropped his head and his voice. "The baby didn't get a coffin. They put her in her mother's arms and buried them together."

A sharp sniffle and Sandra looked away.

Max said, "Did the police ever learn why he did it? It was 1929. The stock market had just crashed. He lost everything maybe and decided to take out his family before they had to suffer? Something like that?"

"If anything, that farm had a lot going for it. As far as I know, nobody ever figured out why it happened. I think he wrote some letters before killing himself, but I don't know what was in them. It was a big story and all, but it didn't really change my life or anything. It was dark and horrible, yet our lives kept moving on."

As Max pulled off the highway and headed toward Trade Street, he said, "Then why are you acting so sad?"

"Well, there's one more piece to this that I can tell you. See, shortly after all that tragedy, one of Lawson's brothers decided to open up the house for tours. Charged people twenty-five cents, if I remember."

Sandra wrinkled her brow. "That's sick."

"The Lawson family wasn't particularly wealthy. They had a lot of funerals to pay for. Plus who was going to buy that house? They had to pay their bills somehow. Probably still owed money on the farm itself. And frankly, I'm sure kids and curious folk were sneaking in to see it anyway. Might as well make a buck or two off it."

Max found a parking space a few blocks up from the office. After he turned off the car, he faced Drummond. "I'm guessing that you paid your quarter and took a visit."

"By that point in my life, I'd already had a few run-ins with the more bizarre things in the world. I don't know if I wanted to see the ghosts of any of those kids, but it would've gnawed at me if I didn't try to find out. I think I needed to see if it was real. None of it could be believed, so I had to check it out for myself."

"Did you see anything?"

"No. I walked through that house, though. Strangest part of it was that being there made the place feel less real. It was like walking through a dollhouse. Marie, oldest daughter, she had been making this cake — raisin cake, I think — and they still had the cake. Put it under a fancy glass cover. Everything was still in the house. Everything seemed staged. Except the blood that stained the floor. Especially the ones next to the basinet. That was horrible. That knocked the reality of it into me like a prize fighter's haymaker. And once that sunk into my head, I could feel the pain oozing off the walls." Drummond removed his hat and ruffled his hair at an unreachable itch. "I should never have gone there. For months after, I felt like part of it had rubbed off on me. I couldn't wash it away. It was a terrible experience."

Max pocketed the photographs. "I'd say this place certainly fits the needs of this tragedy group. So, here's what I'm thinking — I'll go up to the office and do deeper research on Lawson. See what I can find about all of this, so we're not walking into anything blind. Drummond, if you can handle it, you know what I'm going to ask you to do."

"I'll check the Other, but I don't expect to find them. All those innocent kids and their darling mother — they had to have moved on. As for Charlie Lawson, if he acted out of witchcraft or some type of curse, then he might be stuck here or in the Other, but I never saw any evidence of magic in that farmhouse. No symbols, no casting circles, not even a mojo bag or an arcane book. Pain and madness — that's what I saw. But not magic."

Sandra said, "I'll take a look into these tragedy groups. Even if their magic is not real, they certainly think it is. Now that I know what I'm looking for, I should be able to find some references, maybe even some spells. Then I'll go pick up PB and J and bring them home."

Max reddened. He hadn't thought about them. "That's good. I appreciate that."

She leaned over and kissed his cheek. "Just be home for dinner tonight. I'm going to put something together so that the four of us can eat as a family. Don't be late."

As Max headed up to his office, he felt a warm flush at the thought of Sandra preparing a family meal. Then his thoughts drifted to Charlie Lawson. Max could not imagine entering his home later that evening and slaughtering Sandra and the boys. What could have driven Lawson to do such a thing? And not just one child but all of them.

As he opened the office door, the researcher in him looked forward to the hunt for information. But the rest of him loathed finding the answers.

Chapter 9

AS MAX SAT BEHIND HIS DESK to start his research, his head reeled. On one hand, the story of the Lawson family massacre tapped into everything exciting about his job. Researching old and unusual stories with the goal of helping people in the present day — his fingertips jittered as he typed in his initial search. But on the other hand, the person he sought to help was PB. What if Max couldn't save him? What if all his research brought them no closer to stopping the people who sought to hurt him? Max's jaw set as he narrowed his eyes onto the screen.

Unlike the other research that the Porter Agency cases brought his way, this one centered on a famous incident. Max would have no trouble getting information. If anything, the problem would be too much information.

As he brought up one browser tab after another, he quickly saw that he needed several approaches to organize the deluge of material. While he preferred to take handwritten notes — it helped him remember things better — he also brought up a blank document on his laptop that he could build a timeline in. He created a spreadsheet to categorize the different websites and color-coded them for easier access later.

"Look at me," Max said to the laptop. "It's almost like I've done this before."

Once he had everything in place, he dug into the reading. There were firsthand accounts from interviews conducted over the last several decades with neighbors and family members still living until recently. There were news articles and photographs — including the infamous family portrait taken shortly before the tragedy. After a few hours, Max had a fairly clear picture of the way things had happened.

It all started back in 1918 when Charlie and his family moved to Germanton. Everything that followed convinced Max that a curse hounded them. Whether or not that curse was witch-borne remained to be seen.

But in the winter of 1919, Charlie suffered an odd form of arthritis that hindered his ability to fully work the farm. As a result, the income loss prevented them from paying their mortgage, and they lost ownership of the land back to the original owners.

One year later, Lawson's son William died from pneumonia. He was only six. Two years after that Lawson's sister suffered the loss of her baby girl in a fire. Autumn of that same year Lawson's brother Marion, lost his ten-month old son, Chester, through a sudden and unnamed illness.

Despite this series of deaths, the families pushed on. The death of children was not uncommon, but Max wondered how normal it was to have so many deaths within the same family tree.

He pulled up the document screen and outlined all the deaths and their years. Then he picked up his pen and wrote in his notebook further details.

"What I really need," Max told his computer screen, "is to understand why Charlie became a raging, homicidal maniac. What led him to destroy all that he loved?"

By all accounts, he did love his family. He took great pride in them, was a stern disciplinarian, and considered by all to be a fine father. Losing his own children and his nieces and nephews would have been a serious blow to him, no matter how common an occurrence child death had been, but that such things could have propelled Lawson to destroy his own family — Max found it hard to believe. After all, the string of child deaths and the slaughter of his own family happened nearly a decade apart. If he had been so distraught by the loss of the children, he would have acted much sooner.

In fact, the Lawsons didn't even move to the murder site until 1927. Despite having little money and little support for the decision, Charlie bought a hundred and fourteen acre farm on Brook Cove Road in Germanton. Max was even able to locate a record of the purchase — $3200 financed by Wachovia Bank in Winston-Salem.

Charlie thought this would be a fresh start, and Max wondered if he knew he had been cursed. If he had attempted to run away from it through this move. But, Max had to remind himself, not every terrible event could be linked to witchcraft.

In fact, the next hour of research brought Max to a very non-supernatural conclusion. Two of them, actually. Which one would prove the truth, he did not know. And he could see an argument that both, when combined, might have led to the horrible events of Christmas 1929.

Back in '27, Charlie went about digging a basement to regulate temperatures in his tobacco pack house. This new farm was going to be the tobacco farm he had always wanted and a lucrative one at that. While digging that basement, Charlie had an accident.

One day, while working on the drainage of his pack house, he used his mattock — a pickax-type tool — to break up chunks of the ground. Unfortunately, the mattock caught on remnants of an old fence buried under the dirt and brambles. Charlie yanked at it hard and when it broke free, the sharp mattock slammed into his forehead. From that day onward, Charlie was never the same. Though nobody could prove that the head injury had changed him, looking at it now, nearly one hundred years later, Max thought there was a good argument to be made that Charlie had begun to suffer bleeding in his brain.

Pressure changes in the brain caused by bleeding or tumors could drastically alter an individual's personality or behavior. Plenty of documented cases existed to support the idea. But back in the late-1920s — such things were still mysteries. With the benefit of a near-century between them, Max spotted numerous moments to back up a brain trauma argument.

In 1928, for example, Charlie took his haul of tobacco to Winston-Salem to sell. A man accidentally hit Charlie's leg with a cart and injured it. Later, the same man did it again. Charlie burst into a rage. The altercation turned physical, and the man pulled out a switchblade. At that point, without a weapon, most people would have backed away. But Charlie pushed on. The man stabbed him, sending Charlie to the hospital for two weeks.

On its own, the incident suggested that Charlie had an ugly temper. But in the face of so many tragedies previously in his life, Charlie almost never showed such violent behavior. After the head injury, violent behavior became far more common. Bouts of anger also followed.

Further evidence came from interviews with Arthur Lawson — the eldest son that Charlie sent off on an errand to avoid the strong, young man from stopping the murders. According to Arthur, in the time leading up to the Christmas tragedy, Charlie complained of severe headaches and even visited a doctor on several occasions. By the fall of 1929, his behavior had grown worse. Some nights, after everyone had gone to sleep, he would spend hours at the edge of his bed crying.

One night, Fannie found him out in the fields cradling his shotgun, lost in gut-wrenching despair. It got so bad that by November 1929, Arthur would sleep fully-dressed — in case he had to get up in the middle of the night due to his father's dangerous, erratic, and threatening behavior.

In addition to Arthur's accounts, much of these details came from Stella Lawson Boles who was Marion Lawson's daughter and only a young girl at the time. She stayed silent for much of her life, but as her end neared, she wanted to set the record straight.

"And then there's the confessions," Max said.

According to what Fannie told others, on many of these nights when Charlie went off to cry or worse — she got the sense that he wanted to confess something. He never came out to say it, but something nagged at the back of his mind. Nobody knew it at the time, but when Stella finally opened up about what she knew, she dropped a bombshell of an interview.

According to her, she had learned that Marie, Charlie's seventeen-year-old daughter, was pregnant. The poor woman had no idea what to do and may have confided in her mother. While it remained unprovable, the suspicion from many people — including Fannie — was that Charlie was the father. In fact, Stella said that Marie confessed Charlie was the father.

"So, perhaps you killed your whole family to hide your shame. And if you were suffering from brain damage, maybe you thought this was a reasonable way to solve the problem."

Max skipped through the actual day of the murders as fast as possible. From what he read, Drummond had a done a fine job of outlining the terrible event. No need to dwell on it.

However, Max did run a search at the Stokes County Sheriff Department website for records of the murders. But there were none. Nothing directly suspicious in that — oftentimes back in those days, when a new sheriff took office, the old records were lost or destroyed. Max did not know if that practice prevailed today, but he knew a lot of vital information had been wasted away years ago.

He also confirmed Drummond's suspicion that the twenty-five cent house tour had been an attempt to raise money to pay for the farm loan. There were rumors of ghosts in the house, too, but nothing substantiated beyond that. It was too late, anyway. In the 1980s, the new owners of the farm demolished the old house and used what salvageable wood they could find to build a covered bridge at the bottom of a steep driveway. The locals called it the Lawson Memorial Bridge.

Max tried to find the place on Google maps but had no luck. Perhaps in the last thirty-some years the bridge had been destroyed, too.

Rubbing his eyes, he looked up from his laptop. The office was dark. He checked the clock on his computer — 6:20 pm. Damn. He was late for dinner.

Chapter 10

MAX SPED HOME, throwing a litany of curse words at the windshield while smacking his palms against the steering wheel. He had read somewhere that ninety percent of being a good father was simply showing up. Yet he had already ruined that part of it.

By the time he reached the house, his anger had dissipated. Instead, his shame hung on him like a drunkard being bailed out of jail by his disappointed family. He would apologize, but there were no words that could replace his not being there when he should have been.

Entering through the side door, he found Sandra cleaning up the remnants of dinner. The boys had already done their part and gone off to their bedroom. Max flashed a sheepish smile as he set his coat and laptop on a chair.

"You know I'm sorry," he said.

He braced for Sandra's hand to go to her hip and her rapid-fire reprimand to unleash. But instead, she opened her dazzling eyes and offered a sober smile. "They'll be up for a while. You should go talk to them."

Max's stomach dropped. Some childish part of his brain had become convinced that he merely had to apologize to Sandra, and in doing so, his remorse would trickle down to the rest of the household. But, of course, that was cowardice. Sandra was right. He needed to talk to the boys directly.

He glanced down the hall at their bedroom door. He had faced vicious witches, horrible spells, and even death itself — apologizing to two boys should not be so terrifying. Yet as he walked down the hall, the walls stretched further and further in his mind. His footsteps thudded straight up into his heart. He wondered if he would have the right words to say.

After a gentle knock on the door and a noncommittal grunt from inside, he turned the knob. "Hi, boys. Sorry about missing dinner."

J sat on his bed with his back against the wall and read a book. PB crossed his legs on the edge of his bed, playing a videogame — motorcycle racing. Since there wasn't much room to walk around, Max stayed in the doorway.

He went on, "I've been working on all the things PB told us about. I guess I got carried away. Didn't realize what time it was."

In a cold monotone, PB said, "No problem. Appreciate you looking into it."

Max turned his head to J, but the boy kept his face buried in the book. "Well, I should have been here. I truly am sorry."

Neither boy said another word. Max waited a few moments, but they gave him nothing more. Cold as a ghost. He stepped back into the hall, closed the door, and returned to the kitchen. For a few minutes, he simply helped load the dishwasher. Once it was running, he knew he had to at least deal with Sandra. The boys might want to shut him out, but they didn't have to sleep in the same bed with him.

"I didn't mean to get so caught up in my research."

She nodded. "You hungry? There's leftovers."

Max stopped her from going to the fridge. "I don't get it. Are you so furious with me that you're acting pleasant? Why aren't you being angry?"

"Because I know you didn't mean it. I know this is a new phase in our developing family. And all new phases have bumps."

"That's sweet of you to say." He stroked her cheek with the back of his hand. "This isn't just a bump, though. I have to be better. And I'm not. I'm a fraud of a father."

"You are not —" Sandra pointed to an empty chair at the table. "Sit."

Her tone told him everything. He sat. Here would come the anger. Here would come the disappointment he deserved to hear. Because it wasn't simply missing a dinner — plans get messed up all the time. This was their attempt at a family dinner. This was a concerted effort to bring four people living under the same roof together into one unit. That's what he had screwed up. And one thing he knew for certain from his own childhood — there were no second chances. He ruined that dinner, and those boys would never forget it.

"I know what you're thinking," Sandra said as she put together a plate of leftovers.

"That I've let you down. That I've scarred the boys for life."

"You were relating tonight to your own childhood. To the way you felt when your mother would be the one to let you down."

Max squirmed in his seat. Even without magic, she could always get inside his head. She just knew him that well.

She set the plate in front of him. "First thing you need to do is eat. You're never good at making decisions or thinking clearly if you're hungry."

"I don't think I can eat."

"The other thing you need to do is listen. I understand what you're going through. You feel like a fraud because you don't know what you're supposed to feel like. You feel like if you were in a room with a bunch of other fathers, they would take one look at you and know you were an imposter. Sometimes it feels like there's a big flashing neon arrow pointing at your head with a sign that reads *This One is Faking It.* Pretty close?"

"A bit of a bull's-eye, actually." Just hearing her put into words what had been racing around his head made it seem less insurmountable. He wanted to rush across the room and hug her, but she had more to say.

"It's not hard to see it — not when I feel the same way."

"But you're already a fantastic mother. It seems like a natural instinct for you. That's what I'm looking for, I think. I need to find my natural instinct for fatherhood."

"That's not what I mean. And for the record, I am just as frightened as you are about being a good parent. But I'm also trying to be a good witch. It's like I'm on this highway of witchcraft, and I'm trying to build a ramp to another route of the same road — if that makes any sense."

"That makes you feel like an imposter?"

"It makes me feel like other witches won't understand me. It makes me question everything I do."

Max let out a shaking breath. "I suppose it doesn't help when Drummond and I also question you."

Sandra walked over and took hold of Max's hand. "There's no guidebook for this. Any of it. You and I have to forge our own paths. We have to push on through and figure it out as we go."

"We're not just talking about witchcraft, are we?"

With a gentle smack on the side of his head, she said, "Will you look at that? The man might have a brain after all."

She gave him a quick kiss, told him she needed a long bath, and walked out. Max stared at the spot she had just occupied and thought about all she had said. She made it sound so simple — not easy, but easy to understand. He did not get the time to think on it further — the spot he watched shimmered until Drummond appeared in front of him.

The old ghost took a swift glance around the room. "Why aren't you having dinner with your family?"

To avoid having an argument with a ghost that might upset PB, Max turned his attention toward the plate of food. Lasagna. Sandra always made delicious lasagna. Clearly, she had chosen this meal because she knew she did a great job with it and wanted something special that the boys would enjoy as well as Max.

Before he let his thoughts spiral, Max looked back up at Drummond. "Did you find anything?"

"As predicted, none of the Lawsons are in the Other."

"Of course. That would be too easy." Max snapped out his napkin and set it in his lap. "Okay, tomorrow we'll take a little trip to Germanton and see if we can find where the old Lawson farm once was."

"Sounds like a smart move. I'll see you tomorrow."

Raising an eyebrow, Max said, "Where are you rushing off

to?"

"My afterlife doesn't revolve entirely around you and your cases. I've got others out there who like to see me — both living and dead."

"You've got a date, don't you?"

"What can I say? I was never this much of a catch when I was alive. But the ghost me is quite eligible." With a wink, Drummond faded into nothing.

Max picked up his fork, and with a slight grin, he took a bite of lasagna. It was good. Really good. But there was nobody in the room to tell.

Chapter 11

WHEN MAX WOKE THE NEXT MORNING, Sandra had already dressed and eaten her breakfast. She kissed his confused face and busied about the bedroom getting her last things together.

"What's going on?" he mumbled through a dry mouth.

"After you went to bed, I hopped onto one of my witch forums and a great opportunity popped up."

"Opportunity for what?"

"There's a witch down near Charlotte and she's leaving the area. She's pretty old and said that as much as she loves North Carolina — she even said she's lived here since she was five years old — the witch community has become too unstable."

Rubbing his eyes, he said, "I think we had something to do with that."

"We certainly sped up the process. But the more I learn, the more I think it was inevitable. Nothing lasts forever, and the Hulls had ruled for over a century. They could never have kept their power much longer. Grandma Mobley and Mother Hope were destined to destroy each other. Neither one would ever succeed in taking over. So, for this particular witch, she's had enough."

"What does that even mean? She's just going to give up being a witch?"

"Sort of. She said she's no longer going to cast spells or make charms or wards or any of that. She has a daughter in New Mexico. She plans to go hang out there and get into the more spiritual side of being a witch."

"I guess that's good news for us. One less witch to have to worry about."

"That's not the opportunity for me. Because she's moving

away and because she no longer wants to cast spells, she's selling all of her rare books."

That woke Max up. More than any other possession, witches coveted their personal libraries. So many of the books that witches used came in only one edition — only one copy. Though some publishers existed that put out books on the subject of witchcraft, and there were even a few who claimed to put out spellbooks, those texts only touched the surface. And with a dainty, gloved hand at that. The majority of books a real witch wanted, she could only get from another witch.

Sandra shrugged on her coat and shouldered her purse. "I set up a simple breakfast for you and the boys. They should be up in a few minutes. Make sure they get to school on time, and I'll be back early enough to pick them up in the afternoon. Love you."

Before Max could even respond with an *I love you,* Sandra exited the room. By the time he got up from bed, he heard her car backing out of the driveway. The thought flashed through his mind that perhaps she had used these books as an excuse to force Max and the boys into dealing with each other. But no — he saw the excitement dancing across her face. She hoped to snag an important book or two before any of the other witches.

Max rubbed his eyes and forced his brain to start working. He had to get the boys moving, deal with all the parents dropping kids off at school, deal with anything his mother wanted to throw his way when he dropped off PB, and hope Drummond didn't bother him throughout the whole morning. His bladder reminded him that he had other steps to take care of first.

During the process of eating breakfast and getting ready for school, it became evident that J had forgiven Max. Or at least, he understood that mistakes happen and had decided to give Max a second chance. PB, however, showed no mercy.

As they drove out to J's school, the car remained quiet. J had always impressed Max with his ability to read a situation, and he clearly sensed the tension in the car. When Max pulled over at the drop off point, J tried to slip out without comment.

But then he stopped. Sorting through his backpack, he said, "Did you pack me a lunch?"

Max closed his eyes and winced. He heard PB's derisive laugh. "He forgot it," PB said.

Pulling out his wallet, Max grabbed some cash and handed it to J. "Is that enough for school lunch?"

The pity in J's eyes withered Max's hope of getting out of this unscathed. J said, "It'll do." He pocketed the money, swung his bag over his shoulder, and hurried into the building.

As Max pulled into traffic, he figured this would be his only good chance to talk with PB — after all, the boy was a captive audience. Part of him wanted to let it all go cold, bury it away and hope that PB would simply forgive him. But the rest of him warned that to do so meant ignoring a wound — one that would fester until years later when PB would act out and Max would have no clue why. Or worse, PB would end up in jail. All because Max had failed to step up and be a real father.

Swallowing down his fear, Max said, "I'm going to say it again — I'm sorry."

"I already told you it's fine."

"Clearly, it's not fine."

"What? Am I supposed to fall down and bow to you? Tell you that everything is wonderful now that you've apologized for not following through on the thing you promised? Is that it?"

"I know it was important that I be at that dinner, and I know I let you down, but it's not like I was out partying or at a bar getting drunk. I was doing research about things involving your case."

PB bumped his fist against the car door over and over. Max wanted to ask him to stop but thought it better to let the boy get some of his anger out that way.

PB said, "I guess you'll make me go to school again. I'll have to spend the whole day with Grandma Porter pretending to actually pay attention."

"If you don't like homeschooling with her, we can set you back up in J's school at any time. Just say the word and I'll make it happen."

PB gaped at Max. "Are you stupid?"

"Hey," Max said with more force than he intended. "I'm trying here. You want to shut me out, that's your choice. But I'm trying."

"Unbelievable. This ain't got nothing to do with you. I got some crazy people out there who want to kill me, and you are the one shutting me out. You won't let me know what you've learned, you make me go off and pretend that school matters, and you don't come through on the things you promised to do. I don't trust you which means I ain't got anybody fighting for me. Which means I'm probably going to die."

Holy crap, Max thought. The kid was terrified — and rightfully so.

Max's natural inclination was to sit in silence and think things through. But it was his past behaviors that landed him in this trouble in the first place. When it was just him and Sandra, they could handle things however they wanted. But he needed to do something right now — so, he went with his gut.

At the next intersection, Max pulled an illegal U-turn. PB gripped the car door as his eyes widened. "What you doing?"

Max said, "No school today. Or maybe we'll call this a field trip."

With a slight shake in his voice, PB said, "Look, I didn't mean to tick you off. I was just blowing steam. We can go to Grandma Porter's. It's okay."

"You were right. Not about school — that is important, but about this case and the way I've shut you out of it. This whole thing is about you, and you deserve to know what's going on. So, you can come with me today. I'm going to check out an old farm where a terrible thing happened."

From the back of the car, Drummond's gruff voice said, "What's that kid still doing here?"

Max winked in the rearview mirror. "That sound good to you? You come with me to the farm?"

"No, no," Drummond said. "I don't want to have to deal with a kid during our investigation. I mean J is tolerable, but only because he sees me. Besides, how are you going to talk with me with this kid around?"

PB nodded. "Okay. You tell me what I need to do."

"Right now, we get a bit of a drive. So let me tell you everything I found out about the Lawson family."

Despite Max's intention to detail the Lawson story in full, part of him thought it best not to get too graphic. PB was not squeamish and had lived a far tougher life than most, but considering the life-threatening pressure upon the boy, Max did not want to add to it. PB did not need to imagine his own death as anything similar to the Lawson family.

At the same time, Max wanted to keep talking throughout the drive. He did not want to give PB a chance to change his mind. So, he mentioned some of the smaller incidents that had occurred in the build up to the murders. Namely, a strange little side story that had tickled Max when he first read it.

Early on, long before Charlie had the accident that injured his brain, there came to his attention a strange odor coming from his property. People complained to his brother Marion, and it did not take long for Charlie and Marion to discover the source. Protected by a wall of trees, one of the Lawson's other brothers had decided to set up a moonshine still. Charlie was not happy — he was trying to build up his tobacco business and did not need a bad reputation following his product.

PB snickered at the tale, so Max decided to share another side story that involved two people on the lead up to the murders. First, in late-summer 1929, Marion's little daughter, Stella, woke up with a frightening vision of death to her beloved cousins. It shook her awful, but nothing came of it in the following days, and her family dismissed it as a nightmare. But also, on the Christmas morning of the massacre, Joe Lawson — the brother who had a fondness for making moonshine — began to cry uncontrollably at breakfast and continued to do so throughout the day. He could not explain why, but he felt deep to his bone something bad had come over the world.

Max hoped that those two stories would be the start of

leading PB toward the truth about the supernatural. J had come to accept that ghosts existed — hard to deny them when he started seeing Drummond. But PB still thought that the Porter Agency hustled a scam by placating foolish marks who believed in magic and such.

When they drove up Route 8 through Germanton, Max could feel the tension rising. PB stared at the trees and fields with an eager enthusiasm, but his fingers danced on his jumping knees. To Max's eyes, however, he saw little to be either excited or apprehensive about.

The road looked like any rural road with a few houses spaced far apart and plenty of land — some cultivated, some growing wild. As they turned onto Brook Cove Road, Max glanced at Drummond in the rearview mirror. "You see anything?"

PB shook his head, but Drummond checked on both sides of the road. "Nothing that matters," the ghost said. "There are some ghosts around, but there are always ghosts around everywhere — most everywhere, anyway. Nothing stands out as important."

"Well, keep your eyes open."

PB said, "What am I looking for?"

Drummond said, "How about a taxi to take you home, kid."

"I'm not sure," Max said. "That's kind of the nature of what I do. Sometimes you just have to look around and see what pops up."

Following his map program, he found the driveway to what had been the Lawson farm. It was a dirt and gravel road, snug between the trees, and led several acres length away from the main road. Trees surrounded the property, cutting off view of the rest of the world.

Before they reached the current owner's house, Max pulled over. "We have to be careful. We're not supposed to be here. But since what was the Lawson house is no longer around, and the new house was not built on the same spot, I'm hoping we can check out the areas we need to investigate without alerting anybody."

"Plus," PB said, "it's still the morning. Whoever lives here probably is off at work."

"That, too."

Drummond said, "Huh. The kid actually has a good brain. If he keeps thinking like that, I might like him a little better than you."

As they exited the car, Max said, "Stay close. Don't go wandering off."

"I trust you're talking to the boy and not me. And you're right about that — keep a close eye on that kid. A lot of dark things happened here, and evil as a way of sniffing you out."

Despite the shade provided by the trees, the day's heat had already kicked up. Humidity pressed against Max's skin, and even the slight breeze in the air could not cool him. He moved slowly. PB, on the other hand, ignored the heat and started exploring with verve — his curiosity overcoming whatever fears had developed during the car ride.

Max strolled along the gravel drive, keeping an eye on PB while also scanning the area for any signs of where the Lawson house might have once stood. Even with the heat, the place had a soothing, peaceful aura about it. Hard to believe a horrific massacre had occurred here so long ago.

"I'm getting mixed feelings about this place," Drummond said.

Speaking low so as not to alert PB, Max said, "Feelings? That doesn't sound like you."

"I don't mean I'm getting all mushy. But this place has a strength that still holds on to some of the darkness that happened here. It's beautiful and calm, but I still can feel that bad thing."

"I feel it, too. Like being in a bakery but smelling something off mixing in with all the cakes and breads and stuff."

Drummond looked at Max with incredulous impatience. "I swear sometimes your brain makes no sense to me."

Ahead, Max spotted a small clearing. It looked too uniform, too square, to have naturally occurred. "That's it, isn't it?"

Drummond pushed back his hat. "It certainly is. I can

almost hear the gunshots echoing in the air."

"Literally? Or are you just being poetic?"

"Not sure. But I don't think you should let the boy go anywhere near that clearing."

Max turned back toward PB, but the boy had headed off to a string of trees near the bottom of the sloping ground. Max opened his mouth to call PB closer when the boy waved his hands in the air. "Come here," PB said. "I think I found something."

Max and Drummond exchanged a curious look before they headed down the slope. Unable to wait for the old folks to hurry up, PB sprinted uphill toward them. In the thick heat, he dripped with sweat and panted heavily, but that did not stop his excitement.

"Down there. There's a little open area with some rocks for a campfire, and from the story you told me in the car, I'm thinking that's where the moonshine still was."

Max did not know whether to put much faith in that guess, but at least it took them away from where the house at once been. "Let's check it out."

Stepping between the trees, Max saw immediately that PB was right. It made sense for Joe Lawson to put his still there. Not only did the trees provide privacy and protection from people snooping about, but Max could hear the gentle trickle of a nearby creek — accessible freshwater would have made the moonshine business substantially easier.

Hopping around like an eager puppy, PB said, "I'm right, aren't I? This is it. This is where that dude made his booze."

"I think it might be," Max said. "If not, it should have been."

Passing through the thick trunk of a maple, Drummond said, "This was definitely the place. I saw enough illegal setups in my time to recognize a site like this. Even without the equipment, this would definitely be the kind of spot a moonshiner would want — especially if his brother owned the land."

Off to the right, a large rock invited Max to rest. He sat and had to admit that it felt as if many people had sat there previously. The rock beneath him was smooth and perfectly fit the needs of his posterior.

Taking a cue off Max, PB leaned back against one of the trees. With one foot up and pressed into the trunk like some cool kid from the 1950s, he crossed his arms and said, "What happens now?"

"Don't know," Max said. His eyes roved to the ground as he tried to picture the moonshine still from over a hundred years ago. "It would sure be nice if we could magically look under the ground and see if several feet below are remnants of something related to the Lawson family."

With a gruff snort, Drummond said, "Not being subtle, are you? Okay, okay. I'm on it."

Drummond lowered through the ground until only the top of his hat broke the surface. It moved back and forth like the dorsal fin of a shark prowling the shoreline.

"Can I ask you something?" PB said.

"You never need permission. Just ask the question."

"Why is it that you and Sandra try to help people so much? I mean, sometimes you're stringing them along with all that ghost stuff, but even those people, it seems like you're trying to help them, too. I don't get what you're up to?"

"Well, first, good for you for thinking through some of this. Second — I know Grandma Porter can be a bit much sometimes, but she taught me a lot of good things growing up. One thing she sure taught me was that when given the choice of showing kindness or being mean, you'll always benefit more from kindness. Being hateful and mean, spiteful or violent, these things seem like solutions at the time, but they rarely are."

"Yeah, but sometimes you have to fight."

"Sure. Sometimes it's the only way to stop a hateful person. But you shouldn't be in a position where you have no other choice. Because anytime you have another choice, it's better to be kind. Simple as that."

"I guess Charlie Lawson never learned that. Because for some reason he killed his whole family. I can't believe there was no other choice."

"Yeah." Max watched PB's drawn brow and the way he bit his lip. The Lawson story may have been too much to throw at the boy. Max went on, "Whatever the reason that he chose to kill them, he realized later he had made a mistake. Too late, of course, but even people consumed with hate eventually have to face their actions. His guilt over what he did showed in the fact that he took his own life."

Drummond rose from the ground. "This is definitely the spot where the still was. There's some copper tubing and a whole boxful of Mason jars down there. Something else, too. Not far below, there's a ring of stones — and each one has a symbol like the ones we found on that car."

Max's stomach sank. But he had no time to consider the implications because he heard footsteps approaching.

A gray-haired man wearing overalls and carrying a shotgun stepped into the clearing. He rested the shotgun casually on one shoulder. "Good morning," he said, making the words sound more like a threat than a greeting.

PB pushed off the trunk and inched towards the nearest gap between the trees. Max remained seated. In his experience, acting guilty only heightened the threat.

"Morning," Max said with a wave of his hand. "How're you doing?"

"This here is private property."

"Oh, I'm so sorry. We had no idea. You the owner?"

"Caretaker."

"I'm sorry if I caused any trouble. I'm a historian, that's my son, and I was just doing a little research. I'm wondering if I might talk with the owner."

"You may not." In a smooth motion, the caretaker lowered his shotgun — not in a threatening manner but clearly with overtones of threat. "I'll have to see your phone before you leave. Make sure you didn't take any pictures."

"Excuse me?"

"The people that live here care a lot about their privacy."

Max stood and could not miss the man's hands tightening

around the shotgun. "Now look here, I'm sorry this is private property — we didn't mean to cause you any fuss. We'll go back to our car and be on our way. But you have no right to look through my phone."

The old man raised his shotgun. "I'd say I have all the right I need."

"You're going to shoot me? You're really going to kill a man over some accidental trespassing and end up in jail for the rest of your life? Does that make any sense?"

Without a smile on his face, the caretaker said, "I'm sure I could pull together a story that you attacked me. An old man like me being jumped by a guy like you — I think self-defense ain't that hard a case to make."

Max's stomach twisted tight. Before his mind could suggest otherwise, he lunged forward, shoving the barrel towards the sky. "Run," he yelled at PB.

The boy took off like a rabbit frightened by a dog. The old man struggled for control of the weapon. He had more strength than Max expected, and if Drummond had not intervened, Max did not know who would have won. Thankfully, the ghost passed his hand through the man's head — not enough to knock the man unconscious but enough to chill him hard.

"Sorry old timer," Drummond said. "I'd rather knock you out, but at your age, I'm worried you might die."

The caretaker bent over, clutching his temples. Max reached for the weapon, but Drummond said, "Forget that and get to your car."

Max sprinted through the woods. He found PB already sitting in the passenger seat with his seatbelt locked. As he rushed toward the car door he could see PB urging him to move faster. He hoped the old man was not catching up.

Seconds later, Max dropped into the car, thrust his key in the ignition, and tore off down the driveway. Once they hit the main road and were back on Route 8 heading towards Winston-Salem, Max and PB took one look at each other. They burst out laughing.

Chapter 12

PB'S ENTHUSIASM KEPT HIM IN GOOD SPIRITS for the rest of the day. Even when Max dropped him off at Grandma Porter's, he energetically rushed inside to finish the last half-day of school. Max could not hold back his own smile.

Over dinner that night — Max did not dare miss the makeup date for that — PB regaled Sandra and J with tales of the harrowing adventure. "I never run so fast in my life. And I could've sworn we were going to get shot."

"Sounds like you had quite a day," Sandra said in a pleasant tone that did not fool Max. Of course, he understood her concern for PB's safety, but she knew Max could handle things. Surely, she could not blame him for the caretaker's actions. Plus, they had the benefit of a ghost on their side. If anything, he expected her to be happy that he had found a way to connect with PB.

J also sent mixed signals that PB did not pick up on but Max recognized. J said, "Better be careful or you're going to start believing in ghosts like Max."

"Shut up. It wasn't no ghosts chasing us. He was a bad dude with a gun."

"I'll bet there was a ghost with you. You just don't see him."

J sent a knowing look to Max and Sandra. They would have to talk with him soon. Max understood that the boy's jealousy toward PB getting a day off overcame his sense of what he should and shouldn't say, but Max also knew how that kind of behavior left unchecked could turn into something very ugly. They would all have to be careful.

The rest of the meal played out much the same. PB's unbridled excitement bubbled over and he would tell more details of the day. Things that really had not been too thrilling became monumental events building like a symphonic crescendo to the climactic showdown with the evil caretaker. Sandra and J politely listened, smiled and said a few kind things, but neither hid their displeasure either. When the meal ended, Max hoped to get a moment to talk with Sandra alone, but cleanup, homework, and the chores of the evening kept them busy.

Later that night, as they settled in for bed, Max finally had a chance to speak. "Why are you mad?"

Sandra propped up her pillows to read a little. "I'm not. But I am disappointed."

"I thought this was a great thing. I found a way to get PB to talk with me — a little, at least. It was kind of a bonding thing."

"No, what you did was similar to a step-father trying to buy a child's love."

"He needs to be a part of this. He told me so. He wants to feel some control over this insane thing that's happening to him."

"Maybe so. But you went about it the wrong way. Not to mention that involving one of our boys in our cases without consulting me was not smart. But I am not mad. If you or PB got shot, I'd be furious with you. As it is, I think you need to be smarter about this."

Slapping his pillow and rolling to the side, Max said, "At least I didn't miss dinner tonight."

She smacked his back. "How is it that you don't understand? We're usually on the same page with things, yet now that we're all under one roof in a permanent situation, suddenly you don't comprehend being a parent like I do. Why?"

"What did I say now?"

"You don't get bonus points for doing what you're supposed to be doing. Showing up for dinner does not make you a great father."

"But not showing up makes me a bad father?"

"There — now you're starting to understand." She tugged on his shoulder until he turned to face her. "I'm hardly an expert on being a parent. I'm winging it just like you. But I know one thing — we get penalized for doing things wrong and we get zero credit for doing them right. That's part of the deal. When it comes to the Sandwich Boys, that all goes double. They've been let down so many times that the slimmest infraction is going to hurt terribly. And they're going to doubt everything you do right."

Max wanted to scream in frustration, but through a tight jaw, he said, "Why are you mad at me for giving him a good day? Sorry, you're not mad. Just disappointed."

He really wanted to fight with her — have a good, healthy yelling fest. The making up part would be fun, too. Instead, Sandra gazed down at him with all the Southern pity of a woman who had spent her whole life in North Carolina. "Bless your heart, you really don't get it."

"I guess I don't. But I'll tell you one thing — that trip was a success. You may not like that PB came along, but he's the one who figured out where the moonshine still was. Because of that, Drummond found a circle of rocks buried in the ground with the same symbols as the Soro Group. I think we can be fairly certain the next so-called suicide is going to happen there. We just don't know when."

With a cocky wink, Sandra said, "We just might."

Max's pulse jolted into action. "You found something?"

Sandra picked her phone up off her bedside table and searched through her notes. "While you were turning our son into target practice, I've been following up on those symbols. And I found out some interesting things."

"I thought you couldn't find anything out about those symbols. Isn't that why we saw Madame Yan?"

"At first. But afterward, after she told us about the tragedy group and Soro Brown, I was able to go back and dig a little deeper. Plus, when I went book shopping at that old witch's place — the one that's leaving North Carolina — I found a book called *Cults and Lesser Forms of the Occult including Non-Magical Organizations.*"

"Great title. Rolls right off the tongue."

With the light of her phone reflecting against her face, Max caught the corner of her mouth lifting. She said, "The actual book isn't that much easier to read than the title, but I wasn't really looking at it in a *read cover-to-cover* kind of way. I went specifically looking for information on these tragedy groups."

Max sat up. "Are you going to keep me guessing or are you going to tell me what you learned?"

"Hold on," she said, swiping through page after page of notes. "Here it is — so after several pages of explaining why there is no actual magic involved in these suicide ceremonies they're using and how this is all crap that will never actually work, the author goes on to suggest that there might be some validity to it anyway."

"So, they actually are using magic?"

"She says here that in an unintentional way, they may have tapped into some of the natural energies that witches use to create spells. The energy of the tragedy plus the energy of the ceremony — and, unfortunately, the energy of creating another tragedy through these suicides and murders — it is feasible that they might be able to produce a magic spell. Whether they are capable of creating a spell that brings prosperity or power to them is another matter entirely, but something might occur."

"I don't see how that's going to help us figure out when the next ceremony is going to happen."

"That's because you won't shut up and let me talk. Listen — that book on cults says that once the tragedy cycle has begun, it must be performed every third night. As long as the body we found at Odd Fellows Cemetery wasn't the last one in the cycle, then three days from that one there's going to be one more. If it was the first body, then three days after the second one will be yet another."

"Three days?" Max popped to his feet and started pulling on his pants. "That's tonight." As he grabbed his shirt and socks, he froze and stared at Sandra. She had not moved. "What's wrong? Why aren't you getting dressed?"

She rested back against her pillows. "Because we can't both go. Somebody has to stay here with the boys."

Max watched her sitting on the bed as if she floated on a raft and he treaded water in the ocean. Just out of reach — she was floating further away. "No. We're a team. We've got to do this together."

She grinned but it lacked any sense of happiness. "I love you for saying that. I really do. But we're parents now. We have to learn to split our duties between taking care of the boys and running our business. So, tonight, you go out and work on the case. I'll stay here."

"You sure?"

"For tonight. But don't think you're the one who gets to go have all the fun every time."

He walked over and sat on the side of the bed. Holding her hands, he kissed her palms. "I don't know what to say."

"You don't have to say anything."

"I don't know how to be a good father — clearly. And it seems that my knowledge at being a good husband is going to have to shift, too." He stared into her eyes, trying to force her understanding of his love through sheer act of will. "Don't drift away from me. We still have to make it through all of this together. I will figure out my part in it. I will. You just have to give me time."

"I'm always there by your side. You know that. I've been saying all along that we have to learn how to do our new roles in life. That's why I'm not mad at you about any of this."

He pulled her close and wrapped his arms around her. "I don't want you to think I'm leaving you behind."

"Hon, you've got to get a grip on yourself. We're going to be okay. I promise. You'll get better at this father stuff, and the boys will come around. As for me — as long as you keep trying, I've got no complaints. After all, that's part of love. Now, go out there and stop a crazy suicide cult."

Max finished getting dressed and as he headed for the door, Sandra added, "Bring Drummond with you. No reason for you to go completely alone."

"Of course. Isn't that what he's for?"

Chapter 13

THE DASHBOARD CLOCK READ 11:42 PM. Max parked on the side of Brook Cove Road a short distance away from the drive leading up to the old Lawson farm. When he cut the engine and turned off the headlights, darkness engulfed him. No streetlights, no house lights. The town had gone to sleep.

"If I wasn't a ghost, this would be spooky." Drummond drifted out of the car and looked up at the sliver of moon creeping from behind the clouds. "You remember to bring a flashlight?"

Max got out of the car. "I've got my phone. It has a light."

The nonstop buzz of the nighttime insects surrounded them as much as the dark. Though the evening had cooled significantly from the high of the day, it was still hot and humid. Max's shirt clung to his back as he crossed the street and made his way toward the driveway.

Dirt and gravel crunched beneath his feet. He moved as fast as possible without breaking into a run. "Maybe you should go ahead and find out where they are."

"I think I better be here by your side. Just in case something happens to you."

"There's not a lot of time until the witching hour."

"We don't know that's when this is going to happen. Besides, there are a lot of witching hours. I learned that long ago — midnight, one o'clock, four o'clock. Those are the most popular, but frankly, depending on the regions and cultures, you got a witching hour pretty much every hour between midnight and dawn. Let's just focus on finding where they are."

"We know where they are — the moonshine still. I meant for you to go ahead and check out what they're doing, where they're standing. See what I'm walking into."

"Don't worry. I'll go ahead and look. But I'd be a bad partner, if I didn't take care of you, first. That's all I'm talking about. I want to make sure you're seeing things clearly."

"What does that even mean?"

"Well, what do you think is going to happen? I mean if we stop this, do you think that'll save the kid?"

Max wanted to indulge a moment and discuss things, but no matter what Drummond said about the witching hour, Max was not going to take any chances. He sped up his walk. "I don't know. I don't even know what they have planned for PB. If anything, at all. We could be completely wrong about these nutcases coming after him. But we're simply not going to risk it. Even if stopping this ceremony doesn't save PB, it's better than doing nothing."

Drummond threw his coattails back and thrust his hands into his pockets. "You're right about that. Okay, I'll go check out ahead. You keep a move on."

"Thank you," Max said, making no effort to hide his exasperation.

The late hour made everything strange and different to Max's eyes. He only knew he approached the moonshine still site by the sudden slope of the land. At length, he noticed the wall of trees and crouched behind their thick trunks. Cupping his ear, he tried to hear if anyone spoke.

From inside the clearing, Drummond called out. "It's okay. You can come on in. Nobody's here."

Sweat chilled on Max's face. He peeked over his shoulder, half-expecting the caretaker to be standing there with his shotgun. Just the sloping ground and darkness. Licking the salt off his lips, Max scurried between the trees and joined Drummond.

The ghost floated several feet away, hovering over the edge of a circle of stones. Not just any stones — somebody had dug up all of the stones that Drummond had discovered. The odd symbols painted on them were clear even in the limited moonlight. In the middle of this circle, the smoldering embers of a fire smoked into the air.

"We're too late." Max kicked at the dirt. He wanted to kick the stones or pick one up and hurl it into the woods, but he knew better than to mess with a casting circle — at least, not until he understood the spell being cast.

"Calm down." Drummond spread his arms to indicate the entire area. "Do you see a body? Do you see any blood? There's still time."

"You think this is part of the ceremony here and they've moved elsewhere for the suicide? It's possible."

"It's our best bet."

Max spat to the side. "I'll check the old Lawson house. You check the new owner's place."

"I'm on it." Drummond disappeared.

As Max jogged uphill toward the old clearing, his heart pounded. Not from the exertion, but from picturing PB at the mercy of this crazed group of people. When he reached the clearing, he found nothing but empty grass and plenty of nighttime insects.

Drummond appeared next to him. "Owner's place is shut up for the night. Nobody's there. Maybe we're wrong about the Soro Group. Maybe we made a mistake in our thinking."

"You saw that ring of stones. Those embers were still glowing red. We missed something here. Just recently. And as you said — no body. It's not quite midnight — if they're going for the first witching hour, there's still time."

"Well, they're not here. Is there some other tragic location that came up in your research? Maybe the funeral home that put the Lawsons in those caskets in the photo."

Max perked up. "You're right."

"I am?"

"Sort of. The Lawson massacre happened right here, but it didn't end here. Lawson ran down to the river and spent hours circling a tree, trying to deal with what he had done. In the end, he killed himself by the water."

Max closed his eyes and pictured all of his research on the Lawson massacre. He tried to recall the direction of the river and exactly where Charlie Lawson had ended up. Snapping his eyes open, he bolted away from the clearing like a dog on a fox hunt. Drummond soared next to him. As Max weaved around trees and hopped over obstacles, Drummond simply passed right through it all.

In a short time, Max spotted the flickers of firelight up ahead. He stumbled to a halt and crouched. He scurried as close toward the firelight as possible. Hiding behind a large rock, he witnessed a gathering of people, some carrying torches, all wearing ceremonial black robes with symbols painted on the backs. In the center, a young man with terrified eyes knelt before a tall man in a purple robe.

Chapter 14

FOR MAX, eavesdropping on a ritual designed to create magic had become too familiar. He had seen the shadowed figures, the weird symbols, and the flickering firelight before. He knew too well the way they would form a circle and chant as a group. It had all become rather humdrum, and he found himself wanting to fast forward to the parts that diverged from his expectations.

Apparently, Drummond felt the same. "What is it with these people and their cloaks? Just once I'd like to see them all dress like Vegas showgirls or hippy mobsters or —"

"*Hippy mobsters?*"

"You get the point."

The purple-cloaked figure stepped forward with arms raised high. The group lowered their heads and said, "Praise be Soro Brown."

"Praise to you all," Brown said. "Put your faith in me, and I shall lead us all into a world of greatness. Whatever you dream of, it can be yours. All you need is unwavering faith, a true belief in our purpose, and your desires shall be reality."

Max shook his head. "Ridiculous."

"I do not ask you to trust in false promises. I do not ask you to put your faith in a mystical being you cannot see. No. I ask you to judge the evidence of those who have come before you. Those who have worn the cloaks you wear, who have spoken the words you speak, who have witnessed the sacrifices you will witness. They are the proof. Their success, their wealth, their power is the testimonial of all I promise. These nights we spend performing this sacred ceremony are an oath that when we finish, all that we seek shall be delivered just as it has been done for many before us."

Drummond said, "How do people fall for this junk?"

"Shhh," Max said.

"They can't hear me. Besides, if they want to cast a magic spell to get rich and powerful, this is about as far from the real thing as you can get. And what's with that, anyway? I mean, once you accept that magic exists in the world, how difficult is it to find out about the witch community? With a little bit of effort — and I mean very little — these people should be able to recognize this charlatan for what he is."

"People can be blinded easily — especially when somebody starts promising everything you want. They're not stupid. Just desperate enough to believe any lie, no matter how big, as long as it gives them hope that things will be better down the road."

"That doesn't change the fact that these people believe in something fake but every bit as dangerous as the real thing. Maybe even worse because with a witch, you at least get results."

Whispering, Max said, "Then let's go break up their fake spell. We ruin it for them and we'll take away Soro Brown's power over them."

"Not yet." Drummond pursed his lips as he watched the circle of cloaks.

"If Wilson Klein's death means anything, then that poor fool on his knees is going to die."

"We don't know exactly what we're dealing with. If they plan to kill the guy, then they've got weapons. Did you bring your pistol?"

Though he already knew the answer, Max's hand fumbled at his belt. "Um, I forgot."

Drummond gazed up to the sky. "Will you ever start learning from me? Okay, look, you need to think better. Clearly, this whole thing is a bamboozle, but that doesn't mean you should risk your life going in there. You got a wife and two kids to think about."

Max had been thinking about them. The longer he sat back and did nothing, the greater the danger to PB. This group had created a ticking timebomb that Max could not see, hear, or locate. It might turn out to be a dud, but he had to decide how far he would risk everyone before he took the dangerous leap and tried to stop it.

Soro Brown turned in a slow circle and chanted. *"Aca dol shanti tiqua."*

"That's a lot of crap he's serving," Drummond said.

Max agreed. He had come across enough ancient languages from enough authentic witches to know nonsense when he heard it. If this absurd show didn't pose a serious threat to PB, Max would find the entire gathering pathetic and somewhat amusing. But a belief in false magic could be every bit as violent as the real thing. "Maybe I should call the police."

"We don't know if any of those people under the cloaks are the police. Even a good cop can still be lured into a stupid mess like this. Look at Officer Glader moonlighting for Cecily Hull. The promise here is for a lot more money. Odds are that even if none of those folks are police, some of them hold serious power in the area."

"I can't just sit here and do nothing," Max said, his whisper turning into a sharp hiss. "The last one of these ended up with a guy dead in a car by a cemetery."

"Patience. We wait until Brown does something threatening. Until then, we sit tight."

"But —"

"If you go running in there right now, you might end up arrested for disturbing a lawful religious gathering. All they've done is dress up and chant a bunch of made up words. There's nothing here that warrants any action. I know you're worried about the kid, but trust me, you'll be doing more harm than good for that boy if you rush in."

Of course, Max knew Drummond was right. Knew it before the ghost had uttered a word. It had kept him crouched behind a tree instead of taking action. But that did not make it any easier to do nothing like a boy forced to sit in the corner while his classmates ran off to play. Except that the word *play* did not quite fit.

Soro Brown stopped his performance and stepped before the kneeling man. "Kevin Jasper, you are before us with the offer of a great sacrifice. We praise you for this." The group uttered somber words of thanks. "But your gift will not be required. Not tonight. Not ever."

Frowning at these words, Kevin gazed around at the group. Max thought he spotted a glimmer of hope, but the man's fear overshadowed it. Soro Brown patted Kevin's shoulder and guided him to his feet.

"Please, return to the circle. Join your brethren and enjoy all the riches destined to come your way."

As Kevin donned his cloak and hood, he stumbled back to the circle. He looked around as if he expected to be thrown back to the center at any moment. Even as Soro Brown walked in front of the other figures as if playing some mad game of duck-duck-goose, Kevin paled and appeared lost in himself. After several steps, Soro Brown halted in front of another figure and pointed.

"Jackson Wheeler, come kneel before the group."

The man hesitated.

"Come now. You have nothing to fear."

Wheeler did not move.

"A little help," Soro Brown said, and those on either side of Wheeler grabbed the man's arms and escorted him to the center. One of the *helpers* pushed Wheeler to his knees while the other pulled back Wheeler's hood.

He was a young man, college aged, with a shock of curly, red hair that struck Max as so out of place as to be comical. Except the quiver in the man's chin, the open eyes searching for an escape, the shaking of his limbs all pointed to the much darker reality. He had replaced Kevin, and the terrified expressions had come with the job.

Soro Brown stepped before Wheeler. "You have done a great dishonor to this group."

Wheeler bowed his head. "I'm sorry."

"You've betrayed our confidence. Worse, you betrayed our brother and friend, Wilson. Death by his own hand, a tragedy compounded, was a key component of what we are doing here. Without that, our success is doomed. Yet, you disturbed his body. You moved his limbs."

Drummond said, "I told you that Klein was pointing into the woods."

Sniffling, Wheeler said, "I only wanted to —"

"We know what you wanted to do. But each must wait his turn. Casting your little side-spell to jump the line was never going to work. And it could have destroyed our efforts." Soro Brown pulled back his hood to reveal a stern face with an odd yet warm sneer. "You will not succeed in destroying all we cherish. For we are united."

The circle of figures responded like a church congregation. *"We are united."*

"You will not spoil the victories we seek. For we are strong."

"We are strong."

"You will not tear down the fortress of wealth we have built. For we are unstoppable."

"We are unstoppable."

"I have fought too hard, we all have, to let an individual, weak-minded fool ruin the good we have planned. I have spent too many hours studying hard to simply allow you to harm us and our families. You are the one who will be destroyed. For we are invincible."

"We are invincible."

Max wanted to look away but stared on as if witnessing a bad wreck. "This is crazy."

As if an idea had suddenly occurred to him, Soro Brown wagged a finger in the air. "There is one way to redeem yourself, one way to show all in this noble group that you are indeed worthy to be part of us, one way to ensure that those you love will benefit from the greatness to come upon us all."

Wheeler's head lifted, and even from a distance, Max could see the eagerness glisten in the man's eyes. "Please tell me. I'll do anything."

A venomous grin rose on the corner of Soro Brown's

mouth. He stepped closer to Wheeler like a man might approach an animal he considered his own. He licked his lips. "Why is it that you have joined us? When we succeed and wealth comes our way, what is it that you want with all that money? What did you plan for the power you expected to receive?"

Gazing upward forced Wheeler's tears to draw back on his face. "My daughter. She has a polycystic kidney disease and needs a transplant. We can't even begin to afford it. When the time comes, we expect we'll be putting a second mortgage on the house. But if this group succeeds, then we can cover all of it. We can save the life of my daughter. My marriage will remain strong."

Soro Brown put his right hand on top of Wheeler's head. "And the power? What do you plan to do with that?"

"I will use whatever I can to influence this system to become better. So that other families don't have to suffer through the madness that my family has endured. People shouldn't have to choose between the life of their daughter and their homes and marriages."

Resting his left hand atop his right, Soro Brown said, "Those are noble endeavors. Far better than many of us seek to accomplish with our gains. It makes me feel hopeful that you truly regret your betrayal to us all."

"I do. I do."

"Then you understand — our magic works by spilling blood upon a tragic land. A tragedy atop a tragedy. Sin upon sin. We cleanse the wrongs done with the innocent blood of our own." From the sleeve of his cloak, Soro Brown pulled out a curved dagger. He held the blade under Wheeler's chin like a sacred offering. "Spill your blood. Take your life so that your daughter may live. So that your family is forever looked after."

Max stood. "That's it."

"Don't do anything stupid," Drummond said.

"I'm not going to sit here and watch this guy kill himself because they've brainwashed him. It's close enough to murder to bother me."

Max stomped forward, and to his relief, he could feel the cold of Drummond at his side. As he stepped from the trees, the hooded figures turned — not startled, not a jump or even a flinch. Wheeler's eyes lifted from the knife. Soro Brown slowly cocked his head to peer over his shoulder.

"Mr. Max Porter, welcome," Soro Brown said.

Several of the figures brandished handguns and a few held hunting knives. Max halted.

"My name is Isaac Brown, and I want to thank you." Brown turned toward Max. He had a strong, charismatic face, and now that he stood closer, Max could see why many were drawn to listen to this charlatan's sales pitch. With a gentle motion, he had his followers lower their weapons.

Drummond inched closer. "Run away from this. Don't listen to another word he says."

Max suspected Drummond was right, but the fact that Brown knew his name raised Max's curiosity. "Thank me? For what?"

That serpent smile rose again on Brown's lips. "Isn't it obvious? I want to thank you for taking care of my son these last few years."

Chapter 15

IF ISAAC BROWN HAD SAID ANY OTHER WORDS, Max would have most likely turned tail and run deep into the forest. Instead, he crept forward like a mesmerized mark at a carnival show. Several of the cloaked figures parted their circle to allow Max in.

"Um, partner, small problem here," Drummond said.

Max glanced back to see Drummond stuck at the edge of the clearing. Darting his attention from tree to tree, he sought the symbols of a ghost ward but found nothing. Still, Drummond could not break through which meant that this tragedy group knew of actual magic — or at least Isaac Brown did.

Crossing his arms as he searched the area, Drummond said, "I know what you're thinking, and you might be right. But these bozos don't strike me as the kind to know anything about real witchcraft. My guess — the ward is from long ago. Sometime after Lawson killed himself here, I wouldn't be surprised to find out that witches used this place as a sacred site. They probably put on some serious wards to protect it."

That possibility sounded much better to Max's ears than thinking Brown practiced actual magic. But that didn't change the fact that Max stood alone surrounded by guns, knives, and a man claiming to be PB's father.

Isaac Brown clasped his hands behind his back and spoke like a professor giving a routine lecture. "I'm sure you have many questions rattling around in your brain. Chief among them — can you trust the things I say? After all, how could I possibly be the boy's father when, no doubt, he told you I was dead — am I right?"

"Something like that," Max said.

"And how could I be the poor, uneducated father I claim to be when I speak well and clearly have resources?"

"Now that you mention it, I'm curious about that, too."

"Well then, while we still have a little time, let me tell you how it came to be."

Wheeler remained on his knees, and Max stared at the man's face, searching for any sign of an ally. But he found none. The prone man begged Brown with his eyes and repeatedly stifled the urge to cry out.

"Don't worry about him," Brown said. "You should be much more concerned about me."

"See that? That right there tells me you're not PB's father. If you were, your concern would be for him. Like mine is."

"PB? Is that what he calls himself? Well, allow me a moment to show you why I am his father. Because I've done everything a great father should do for his child — even if in the end, PB never appreciates me for it."

Max knew he should keep his mouth shut, but he could not help himself. "Abandoning your family, letting your son think you were dead, heck, letting him live on the streets — father of the year material, if I've ever seen it."

Fury flared in Brown's eyes, but he tamped it back with a merciful, patronizing shake of the head. To his followers, he said, "Exactly like I told you. Nobody understands us. Nobody recognizes the horrible sacrifices we make. But that's okay. We have each other. We do what we must, and we never cross the line. We never take pleasure in sacrifice. For we are united."

The group enthusiastically said, *"We are united."*

Brown turned back toward Max. "About ten years ago, I struggled to make ends meet for my family. Gene — that's PB's real name — was a fun kid, and I loved him very much. His mother was a wonderful woman, but she was weak. The life of a poor person is not easy, and Gene's mother could not handle it."

"His name is PB. You better start getting used to that."

Max expected to be hit or stabbed or worse for mouthing

off, but Brown simply nodded. "I suppose you're right," he said as he continued pacing. "PB's mother dealt with our difficulties the way too many do. Drugs became her method of escape which created many more problems in our life. It was then that I heard of the Soro Group. They made a lot of bold claims, none of which I believed — what sensible person would? — but underneath the ceremony and magical claptrap, I spotted a kernel of truth. The idea that if we could all work together, we could benefit each other. This small group could help its members step higher and higher up the ladder simply by pooling our successes. That's what got my attention."

Drummond pressed against the ward like a child with his face against a glass window. "Keep your mouth shut now. You egged him on enough and he's on a roll. Keep your eyes open for an escape."

If Max had stood someplace else, he would have laughed. The idea that Drummond thought he had been mouthing off as part of a grand plan to get Isaac Brown to divulge secrets only hit Max with a darker truth — that he had stumbled into a deep hole and had only made it worse. The sickly sweat clinging to Wheeler's face spoke volumes more of the danger Max faced then the half-raised guns.

Brown continued, "There comes a point in a father's life when he must decide to risk the things he has in order to get the things he wants. I wanted the money and power to give my son and wife a fantastic life. And I have always been willing to sacrifice whatever it took in order to achieve this."

"So, you started giving this group what little you had left? That seems kind of stupid to me," Max said.

"It would've been, if the group didn't work. But it does. The rituals actually serve their purpose. The leader of our group back then was a man named Harris Coleman. He took me under his wing. He educated me. Opened my eyes to the possibilities when we all work for each other. I remember the day when he offered to teach me how to run the group, to prepare me to take his place. I remember it well because I had to make a sacrifice in order to gain that success — I had to allow my family to think I was dead."

Trying to act as if the guns and knives meant nothing to him, Max placed his hands in his pockets and kept his focus on the ground. "I'm guessing your friend Coleman told you that someday your family would enjoy the riches you expected to have."

"If I did things the right way — yes. But I did not. I found a faster route. I pushed him out of power and took over the group."

"Why? Why not wait a little bit longer until he retired?"

Brown sauntered close to Max and leaned in. Speaking softly, he said, "I met an old woman who claimed to be a witch."

A bolt of icy fear shot through Max's chest. Brown took one step back, and the mad look in his eyes created doubt — did the man truly know about witches or was he insane?

"It's true," Brown said. "She showed me the history of these tragedy groups and that they were based originally on real witchcraft. I know it sounds impossible, but it's all real. I also know that you believe me. Because I've been watching you. Don't look surprised at that. You've been taking care of my boy. You had to expect I'd keep my eye on you."

Max had considered it over the last few years, but when PB told them of his father's death, Max's concerns turned only to J's history.

"This witch — who was she?"

Brown shrugged. "She never gave a name. I never asked. She was a peculiar little woman, though. Lived in this amazing underground apartment."

Madame Yan. Max filed that bit of information away for later.

Brown resumed his path around the inner circle. "I used the knowledge I received to build up this group, to teach them the ritual, the real one, the one that works, and we did our research. The witch warned me to keep much of the pomp in the ceremony, that I would only botch the spell if I tried it outright, and I listened. Now we have begun the process that will result in what this group always promised. Now, the sacrifice I made ten years ago can be rectified. I can actually achieve what I've sought, and with luck, share that with those I love."

Brown cut across the circle to stand directly behind Wheeler. "But I gain nothing if blood is not spilled on this tragic land."

Wheeler's shoulders trembled as he bowed his head. Gasping as mucous dribbled off his mouth and nose, he said, "I'm sorry. I can't. I want to. I truly want to help. But I can't."

A sharp motion from Brown brought two of his followers forward. They grabbed Wheeler's arms and held him tight. He screamed out.

"Leave him alone," Max said. "This is wrong. You're playing with powerful forces that you do not understand."

"You think I'm *playing* at this?"

From behind, Drummond called out, "Go. Now. Run."

Caught up in Brown's story, Max had missed the opening that had been created. But the opportunity still remained. He took one step toward the gap left by those who held Wheeler. But he stopped.

"Don't do this," Max said. "He doesn't want to be part of your group anymore."

"That is not what he expressed to us," Brown said. "I know you were listening. I know you heard him. He wishes to save his daughter's life. He said he was willing to sacrifice for his family. He would hardly be the first person to lose his willpower at the crucial moment. It is why the Japanese had the honorable position of being second to a man about to commit *seppuku*. We as a group, as a united group, we will serve as Wheeler's second."

Wheeler struggled against those holding him, and a third person stepped forward. Placing a knife in Wheeler's right hand, the person wrapped tape around it, securing the knife in place. Ignoring Wheeler's tears and whimpers, they forced his arm across his body, setting the blade at the left side of his neck.

Max wanted to dash forward, bulldoze through these horrible people, save Wheeler, and escape. Part of him wanted to ignore all of it and follow Drummond's plea — simply run off and save his own skin. He stood. Frozen.

Brown circled around Wheeler and crouched. "You still have a chance to do this with integrity. Shed your blood and save your family."

Sweat and tears blended into an incessant stream down Wheeler's face. His ragged breath matched the convulsions of his body. He inhaled long and slow, coughed and sputtered, and attempted to breathe in again. Max could see the man mounting the strength for one final act.

"No!" Wheeler's fierce howl cut across the night air.

Max's shoulders dropped. No matter how loudly Wheeler protested, it was over. The disappointment on Brown's face confirmed it.

Brown straightened, glanced at those holding Wheeler, and gave a curt nod. They forced Wheeler's arm to move from left to right, and in doing so, brought the blade across his throat.

The rest happened fast. The blood poured out like thick soup spewing from the side of a cracked bowl. As the dark liquid soaked into the ground, the cloaked figures rejoined hands to make their circle. Brown raised his head and chanted more words of nonsense.

Max stood in the center of it all. He tried to put things in some kind of sensible order. But none of it made sense. How could Madame Yan have given them the secrets of witchcraft yet here they stood chanting gibberish? How could he bring about the safety of PB? Worst of all, how could he get out of this?

He saw only one answer, and he did not like his chances. But before Max could throw his first punch, Isaac gestured to the group and said, "It is done. We have taken one great step toward our future. We have done all that is required, taken no pleasure, and we have gone no further. Be proud of what you have braved. Go home, now. Go home and rest and prepare."

The group lowered their heads and simply filed off into the woods. Their task complete, they did not care to remain around.

Last to exit, Isaac Brown stopped and gazed back. "What? Expecting me to kill you? I am no monster. Only a man with the ability to help those of his flock. We do not relish the hard things we must do, but we understand the necessity."

"I don't. Care to enlighten me?"

"I am sorry that you had to see all of this. I'm sorry that I rambled on about my lackluster life leading up to this point. But, you see, all my talking has served an important purpose. A crucial step that means more to me than a childless man like you could ever know. I needed to give my people plenty of time to break into your home and get my son back."

He grinned as he slid into the dark woods.

Chapter 16

MAX FLOORED THE GAS, flying down the empty rural roads, as he headed toward Winston-Salem. Isaac Brown's vicious face floated in his mind. Over and over, Max saw cloaked figures smashing into his home, confusion and screams, and the roar of PB as they stole him away.

Max had to stay focused. Getting in a car accident would not help. But his blood pumped through his body faster than the gas rushing through his car. He could not clear his mind.

Even knowing that Drummond had flown ahead gave Max no solace. No matter what horror his partner might find, being dead limited Drummond's ability to do anything in this situation.

When Max finally reached the edge of the city, he slowed the car. He could not afford to waste time being pulled over for a speeding ticket. And if by some obscene chance the officer turned out to be Glader, Max would lose all control — probably get arrested on assault charges.

Focus. Drive and focus. Throughout the trip, he tried to call Sandra on his phone but to no avail. He tried once again — still no answer.

When Drummond finally appeared in the passenger seat, relief and terror flooded Max's system. If the two emotions could have used him in a tug-of-war, they would have shredded him in half. "Well?" he said.

Drummond brought his hat down — not a good sign. "Sandra and J are tied up in the bathroom. They're shaking, but they're fine."

"And PB?"

"No sign of him."

Max clenched the steering wheel. "Go back to the house and watch over Sandra and J until I get there."

"On it." Drummond vanished.

As Max hovered around the speed limit down Route 52, his mind replaced terror-filled images of Sandra and the boys being tortured with terror-filled images of PB's pain and hopelessness. The poor boy had been through more than most people in his short life, and now he had to deal with being kidnapped.

Max considered contacting the police. If they put out an Amber alert, maybe they could capture Brown and his group before any harm came to PB. Not that he expected PB's father to be physically dangerous to the boy, but the mental damage would last for years. Perhaps the rest of the boy's life.

As he pulled into the driveway, Max saw the side screen door hanging off its hinges. He hurried inside. Wood from the splintered door jamb spread across the floor, and parts of the deadbolt sat in one of several cooking pots also on the floor. No sign of the rest of the door knob, but a six-inch chef's knife stuck half-buried in the wall. Max swallowed back the urge to throw up as he barreled straight for the bathroom.

Sandra and J looked up with fearful eyes. J had been tied to the sink pipes and a sock had been used to gag him. Sandra had been forced onto her stomach so she could be tied around the toilet plumbing. Mascara ran black over her cloth gag.

Holding back his tears, Max dove forward and worked at J's bindings. After releasing them both, the three sat on the bathroom floor and hugged each other. Sandra cried more, and J buried his tears into Max's shoulder. Drummond waited, floating in the doorway, and respectfully let them cling to each other.

At least five minutes went by before they could muster the strength to stand. Max escorted Sandra to the living room couch and J held tight to her pant leg. Max poured a stiff drink. Nobody spoke as they let the alcohol do its job.

"Can you talk yet?" he asked. "I hate to push you, but every minute takes PB further away from us."

Rubbing the chafed skin on her wrists, Sandra said, "It's not like that. The danger's already gone."

"What does that mean? How? PB is —"

Drummond said, "Just let her talk."

Max whirled toward the ghost. "My wife and one of my boys were attacked, and the other one has been kidnapped. Why should I be calm and take my time?"

"Because all your prancing about and screaming is getting you nowhere." Drummond slipped low into the floor so that his head was level with Sandra. "Tell us what happened."

She looked at J's astonished face as he stared at Drummond. She said, "I was in bed. I assumed the boys were asleep. I heard a banging at the side door."

"That woke us up," J said.

"I went into the kitchen to turn on the outside light, and that's when they came in. They ripped the screen door back and kicked open our kitchen door." She lowered her head into her hands. "I don't know exactly what all happened after that. I threw anything I could at them. I ran to get the boys —"

J said, "We came out and saw them. Two big guys."

Max put an arm around J. "Did they hurt you?"

He shook his head. "PB stopped it all."

"PB?"

"He walked right up to them and told them to stop. He said that there wasn't no reason to hurt me and Sandra. Said he'd go with them and cause no fuss."

Drummond floated backward. "He knew they had come for him."

"Yes, sir," J said. "The minute they started banging on the house, PB and I woke up. He looked right at me and said the people who killed his daddy had come to pick him up."

Max leaned forward. "PB's father is not dead." To the shocked expressions, he explained what he had observed in the woods near the Lawson house.

As Max crossed the room, as he pulled his thoughts together, he had the uneasy sensation of being watched. A lot of good that did him now. He should have been paying attention to that kind of sensation for weeks now. Maybe then PB would be sitting here instead of held prisoner.

He dug the palm of his hand into his forehead to stave off these unhelpful thoughts. "We need a plan. We need to figure out how we're going to get PB back. Doesn't matter that he went with them willingly. He did so to protect you two. Now, it's our job to protect him."

"Of course," Sandra said.

Thinking as he spoke out loud, Max said, "If we all do our part, if we work together, I know we can get him." Nobody challenged his words, but he suspected they all knew he spoke for his own benefit. To Drummond, he added, "We could use all the ghost help we can get. Do you think your network of contacts might be willing to scour the state searching for him?"

"I can certainly ask. I'm sure some of them will be happy to help."

Before Drummond left, J waved his arms. "Don't go yet."

Checking with Sandra and Max before he answered, Drummond looked down at the boy. "You're a brave kid. I don't scare you?"

"You don't scare them. Y'all talk to each other — why should I be scared of you?"

"Kid, every time you speak, I like you a little more. I need to go looking for your brother. So what is it you want?"

"Stay here a minute." J darted out of the room. They could hear him rummaging in his bedroom. Max gave Drummond's inquiring look a shrug as they waited.

A moment later, J returned holding a photograph Sandra had taken of the Sandwich Boys arm in arm after a fun day at Wet 'n' Wild in Greensboro — closest they had gotten to the beach. Offering the photo, J said, "You need something to prove that you're not a stranger. Otherwise, PB will never believe you — nothing you say will matter."

"It's good you're thinking, but PB won't be able to see or hear me. If I find him, I'll have to come back and tell Max or Sandra — or, I guess, I can tell you."

Pushing the photo further in the air, J said, "Please. Take it."

Max had rarely seen the honest grief Drummond held in his face. "Sorry, kid. I touch that, and I'm going to be in a world of hurt."

"I'll explain it to J," Max said and put the photo in his pocket. "You get going. See what you can find."

Drummond gave J a wink before vanishing.

Max turned to speak, but Sandra had already left the room. She returned with a bag on her shoulder and her car keys. "J and I are going to the office. I'll see if I can locate PB with a spell."

"Spell?" J said.

"You're smart enough to understand that ghosts exist. Did you really think it all ended with that?"

J looked from Sandra to Max to see if they were joking. "So, we got magic spells, too?"

"Come with me, sweetie. I'm going to teach you about the world of witches."

Max waited until the two had driven off. He marveled at the strength both Sandra and J had displayed. They had been assaulted and bound to a bathroom, yet they mustered the courage to get working in order to save PB. Max needed some of that same courage.

A fly buzzed a haphazard path above him. It smacked into the windows, changed course, and weaved across the air. Max stood in the middle of the living room listening to that incessant droning and became aware of how empty the house now felt. After all these years with only Sandra by his side, years when an empty house felt comforting like a favorite blanket, now he feared losing one of its new members. Now having less people surround him made the house echo — even with just the sound of a buzzing fly.

No. He refused to let anybody take apart this family they were trying to build.

Two ideas sprang to mind. Neither one struck him as particularly appealing, but he knew he had to follow these routes. After all, Cecily Hull and Madame Yan were the two women that put Max and his family on this path. And he had no doubt that both women would be wide-awake at two in the morning.

Chapter 17

BY THE TIME MAX REACHED MERSCHEL PLAZA, the clock on his dash read 2:27am. He found a parking spot three blocks away and paused to rub his puffing eyes. Like happiness, anger could only be sustained for so long. It drained the body and poisoned the mind. He needed to be sharp and steady. Instead, his adrenaline rushes had crashed and left behind a hollow deep enough to be filled by all his fears.

The one shining light that charged him like the sun reawakening his soul — PB. Knowing that boy sat somewhere tied up, praying for Max to save him, filled Max with all the energy of the world.

Max holstered his weapon — he remembered it this time — and marched down the sidewalk. The weight of the weapon on his belt warned him of the dangers he faced. Especially because he had yet to actually load any bullets.

He did not bother going to the lobby entrance, and instead, headed straight for the side alley that led to the brick-painted door. A different lackey had sentry duty that night — a black woman with a muscular frame and the stance that promised she knew how to take care of trouble. Max wished Drummond had come along with him — the ghost could freeze the guard's head and make entering easy.

With no time to waste, he pulled out his handgun and pointed it straight at the woman. He hoped no police were patrolling the area. "Open the door. I'm going to see Cecily Hull. I'm not here to shoot her or cause her any harm. I just need some information from her."

The woman showed no fear, no surprise, not even a hint of concern. Max might as well have been pointing his gun at a tree trunk. She stepped forward, closing the distance, and rolled her shoulders back.

"You're that Porter guy. I was told about you."

"You knew I was coming?"

"Just that I might someday see your face around here."

Thrusting the weapon forward to emphasize his words, Max said, "I don't care if she knew I might come or what you were expecting. Open that damn door."

She smirked. "You'd be far more threatening if the safety was off."

If she wanted him to look and then take advantage of his distraction, he would disappoint her. No reason to look at the safety when he knew the weapon had no ammunition. However, a gun did not require bullets to still be a dangerous weapon.

Max took one step forward and smashed the butt of the gun against the side of the guard's head. He finally saw some shock on her face. She dropped to one knee. Max had intended for her to be knocked out, but the movies had let him down once again.

Long ago, he had learned how difficult the one punch knockout could be. Getting knocked out with a single hit from a metal object — apparently also difficult.

But she was dazed. Pushing back to her feet, she tried to grapple with him. She had strength and skill, but the blood dribbling down the side of her face and the wobble in her stance gave Max all the opportunities he needed.

From his back pocket, he pulled out two zip-ties. Though she offered some resistance, he managed to get her arms behind her back and tie her wrists together. "I'm real sorry about this," he said as he reached into her pants pockets. He found the keyring he needed and opened the side door.

Once inside the stairwell, he zip-tied her to the railing. Using some strips of an old shirt he had in his car trunk, he gagged her before heading upstairs. The five flights went by quickly and he did not bother knocking on the door at the top.

Max stormed down the corridor with tan fabric-covered

walls. "Cecily Hull. I know you're awake. Evil like you never sleeps."

He tried every door he came upon. They were all locked. When he reached the end of the hall where he expected to open the door to her office, he found another locked door. The rage firing within raced through his legs as he thrust kicked the door knob. It did not budge.

"Mr. Porter," Cecily Hull's crackling voice came over a hidden speaker. "If you insist on damaging my property, I will be forced to call the authorities."

Like a trapped animal, Max tramped down the hall and back again. "You went too far. Involving my boys was a dumb mistake. Cut out the theatrics and meet with me."

"If something has happened to your boys, I can assure you I had nothing to do with it."

"Then why are you hiding from me?"

"Because you are raving mad. If you wish to speak with me like a sensible adult, I suggest you gain some composure. Only then will any of these doors open. Except the one you came through — you are more than welcome to leave that way."

Max halted in front of the office door. He closed his eyes and attempted to calm his frayed emotions. He did not open his eyes. He kept his muscles still. Like a monk deep in a meditative trance, he slowed his racing heart. He refused to give her any reason to remain behind locked doors.

When he heard the click, he summoned all the self-control he had left not to burst through that door, grab her by the neck, and throttle her for answers. Though his fingers shook as he clasped the knob, he managed to open the door with some semblance of grace.

Cecily Hull set behind her stylish desk wearing a blue silk robe that glistened like water under the lights. Approaching faster than he had intended, he said, "You hired me to look into one murder, and I do not believe for a second that you didn't know where it would lead me. Now that freak Brown has gone and stolen PB from my house. He assaulted my wife and my other son, J. This is on you."

As if entertaining a casual business meeting, Cecily gestured toward a chair for Max to sit. When he remained standing, she said in a restrained tone, "Sit down, Mr. Porter."

Had she yelled at him or had she used her normal, clipped and forceful tone, he would have blustered on with his demands for answers. But this — this voice caused his knees to waver. He did not sit so much as fall into the chair.

"I'm not without sympathy toward your situation. Though I am not a parent, I have had people in my charge from time to time. And whenever we have somebody become our responsibility, there is an inevitable bond that forms. So, you are forgiven for your behavior up to this point." She placed her hands calmly on the table, yet that simple gesture turned his stomach. "Now you are expected to behave with respect and caution. Do I need to explain myself further or are you in your right mind enough to comprehend the situation in which you have placed yourself?"

Max found it difficult to swallow. He nodded and sat back to show he would remain calm — he would try, at least.

"Good." She tapped her fingernails on the glass desk. "It is stunts like this that make me look forward to the day when I no longer need your services. You are far too erratic for this business."

"I'm damn good at my job. But you set me up and whether you intended it to happen or not, the result is that one of my boys has been kidnapped."

"And that is unfortunate, but again, I had nothing to do with it. In point of fact, I knew nothing about the extent to which these murderous groups have been operating. After all, that is why I hired you. I wanted to know how greatly I had to be concerned about these tragedy groups." The disdain slithered off her lips.

Max observed her face and her behavior for any sign of deceit. He found none. His legs regained their strength. He had the sudden urge to bolt from the office, sprint down the hall, and jump the five flights of stairs until he could break free from this building. He remained seated.

Cecily went on, "I can see in your eyes that you're starting to understand. Perhaps you are regretting having ever agreed to work for me. That's okay. I am starting to regret ever hiring you. But since the hour is late and I do not wish to have you in my presence any longer than necessary, let me first say that this is not how we do things anymore. Kidnapping and other distasteful crimes are not tolerated by this organization. The norm for the Hull Corporation will no longer involve an old and outdated mobster mentality."

"What about Madame Ti? Are you saying the Hulls are no longer going to play with magic?"

"Oh, I will keep a tight leash on that witch and the power she wields. But all the Machiavellian games my predecessors played are not my way. Neither is your blustering and bombastic method of handling things. I am not here to help you. I am not here to serve you. Your relationship with me and the Hull Corporation is no longer anything even close to an equal footing. Because *this is not how we do things anymore.*"

She let the words hang in the air. Max half expected a cloud to form over his head and strike him with lightning. Finding the will to stand, he said, "Clearly, I've made a mistake. I've kept you up and I should be going."

He managed two steps before she spoke. "Mr. Porter, you're forgetting something."

He turned back. "Ma'am?"

"Don't you think you owe me an apology?"

"I am deeply sorry. As you said, I've formed a strong bond with the boy, and the fact that he is missing has made me think in an unwise manner. Please, forgive me."

Slowly, Cecily Hull shook her head. She placed out her right hand and wiggled her ring finger. "Respect. Remember?"

She let her hand hang in the air until Max understood. A short laugh escaped his lips, but she showed no signs of humor. Cocking his head to the side, he opened his mouth, ready to unleash a harsh word or seven. But the look in her eye stopped him.

Frowning, he walked toward the desk. His face must have

read the question bouncing through his mind — *are you serious?* — because she nodded. She did not smile nor did she raise her head with condescension. She truly wanted him to offer this gesture of respect as if it meant something.

Part of him wanted to turn his back on her in dramatic fashion and storm off. But he had to think about PB. Bowing over her ring, Max said, "I truly am sorry."

"Kiss it." Not a mocking tone. In fact, he could hear no pleasure in her voice at all. To her, it seemed that this was a solemn and necessary act.

Max's lips clamped shut. He fought his brain, bent lower, and focused his thoughts on PB. He kissed her ring. Heck, he would have danced a jig or sang an aria if she had required it. Anything to get out of that office and back to his search for PB.

She withdrew her hand and settled back in her chair. "You may leave now. Let us both hope we never have to work together again. But if we do, I expect you to remember the respect you have learned to show me."

Max turned away and shuffled out of her office. By the time he reached the bottom of the stairs, a second sentry had cut the guard's zip-ties. She looked like she wanted to kill Max in a deliberate and painful manner, but held back. She probably feared what her employer might say.

Max picked up his pace as he headed toward his car. Because if Cecily Hull could be believed — and he did not peg her to be a liar in this instance — she knew nothing about Isaac Brown or the kidnapping of PB. Which left Max with an even less desirable visit that night.

Madame Yan.

Chapter 18

MAX CREPT DOWN RAINBOW STREET, his car wheels grinding the dirt and gravel like a prowling predator. He parked the car in front of Madame Yan's yard and waited. A lamp in the living room window cast an amber glow giving the house a cozy feel in the moonlight.

Max's system was shot. Between the repeated adrenaline rushes, the threats to his life, and the unending, stomach-churning fear for PB, he found it difficult to pull upon any more strength for the coming confrontation. His tank felt nearly empty.

As he ambled toward the front door, every step brought his weight to the ground as if he might continue down until his head rested on the grass and his eyes closed for the next twelve hours. He slapped his face. Twice.

Entering the house, he eased into the living room and waited for Cheryl-Lynn. A full minute went by without anybody showing up. Stepping outside, he pressed the doorbell and then returned to the living room.

No answer.

"Hello?" His voice sounded awkward and foolish as it died against the heavy furniture. He knew they were watching him. Listening. Cheryl-Lynn ran a strict house on behalf of Madame Yan. If she had to go to the bathroom, she would arrange for help to watch the door. Never would the front be abandoned for this long.

Which meant they were making him wait on purpose. That sent ripples of worry for PB throughout Max — they were wasting his precious time. Just as fast, worry turned to anger. They were playing with PB's life.

His hand reached for his weapon, but he held back. No good would ever come from that kind of behavior. Waving a gun around in a person's house would only get him arrested. Waving a gun around in a witch's house might result in an even worse outcome.

But something had to be done.

At the point when Max contemplated barreling downstairs and forcing his way to Madame Yan's underground apartment, Cheryl-Lynn appeared in the kitchen. She tucked a few loose strands of hair beneath her hijab as she approached him. All her quaint charm vanished as she said, "You need to go on home."

"What I need is to see Madame Yan, and I'm not leaving without that happening."

"You do not make demands of her."

"You have no idea how pissed off I am. Madame Yan has the opportunity right now to meet with me and talk things over. But if I leave here without seeing her, she will have made me an enemy. And if she thinks lightly of that, then you best remind her of Mother Hope, Grandma Mobley, and Doctor Connor — to name just three witches who are all gone because of me."

Of course, Max did not directly destroy any of those witches, but he had a hand in the overall environment that led to their demise. If it got him an audience with Madame Yan, he would take whatever credit he needed.

Cheryl-Lynn paused — perhaps giving credence to his words — and finally walked over to the small table with her laptop. "Let me see her schedule. I think I can fit you in tomorrow around —"

"You're not understanding. I'm going to see her right now."

"Do you know how late it is? You know she's been sick — needs her rest. You clearly need it, too. Why, you should be home getting shuteye before the sun comes up."

"I'll wake her if I have to."

She watched him carefully. He got the sense that she only now saw the desperation in his face. Or perhaps the anger.

Whatever the case, she relented.

Stepping aside, she gestured toward the kitchen door that led down to the basement. "She's waiting for you."

Max hesitated. "Waiting?"

"Bless your heart, you really think so little of her. She probably knew you were coming to visit days before you even decided to come."

Max moved toward the door, but Cheryl-Lynn remained by her table. "You're not going?"

"Don't you know the way by now?"

They locked eyes, but Max scowled. He had no time for these games. He walked to the kitchen, his shoulder bumping her further aside, and headed downstairs.

Hastening his pace, Max scurried to the false basement. He pushed open the hidden door, rushed the old stairs, and crouched as he scuttled across the dank, true basement. Twice he bumped his head on the low ceiling as his desire to get to Madame Yan overcame his slow-crouched gait.

"Madame Yan," he called out as he yanked open the door.

One step in and the world flipped on him. He barely had time to register what he saw — Madame Yan sitting in a casting circle surrounded by flickering candles. She had her left hand out and it glowed with a symbol — three lines crossing at odd angles. But even as that image filtered through his mind, Max lifted off the ground, flipped in the air, and landed with his back on the ceiling. He tried to move but felt as if a giant pinned him there with an oversized hand.

"You are not welcome here," Madame Yan said, her voice strong and grave. "Not tonight."

He tried to speak but had to clear his throat twice before he could utter a strained, groaning sound. "I take it your helper upstairs stalled me long enough for you to get this spell going."

Madame Yan glanced upward. "That's why I pay her so well."

"Let me down. Please. I just came to ask you a few questions."

"At nearly four in the morning? You bullied your way into

my home, blasted down here like a madman, and burst into my apartment as if you were expecting to threaten me. That seems like more than just a couple of innocent questions to me."

"Don't be a bitch." Despite his anger, his foul language sounded as impotent as his ability to get off the ceiling.

Madame Yan snickered. "All out of witty retorts, I see. That's a shame. Your smart-alecky mouth was one of the few endearing qualities you had."

"Don't you even care that your meddling is going to hurt an innocent boy?"

"Meddling? I don't even know what you're talking about."

Max wailed and thrashed about on the ceiling, but his body barely moved. "None of your deceit. You knew that Isaac Brown was PB's father. You had to know. You're the one who set Brown onto all of this. You taught him about actual magic. Witchcraft. And when your luck turned that we showed up here, you sent Sandra and I down that same path. On purpose. What are you after?"

Madame Yan snapped her glowing hand into a fist. Max felt his stomach tighten. She then slammed her hand onto the floor, and the hold on Max disappeared. With nothing locking him to the ceiling, he fell.

He managed to curl into a ball before hitting the hard ground. Though his bones remained intact, he knew there would be bruises all along his arms and legs — little purple-black reminders that Madame Yan was more than a doddering, amusing old woman. She was a witch through and through.

"Now then," she said as she perched on one of her stools. "You rushed in here, intent on threatening me, you've spoken obscenities toward me, and now you suggest that I somehow masterminded harm that is coming to your boy. Let me ask you this — if I did indeed cause all of this to happen, why would I help you now?"

Wincing as he sat up, Max crossed his legs and rubbed his sore arm. "Why do any witches do what they do? You're all caught up in your own nutty machinations." He thought of PB and his chest filled as he bowed his head. Tears welled in his eyes. "I just want my boy back."

Madame Yan hopped off the stool. When Max flinched, she smiled. She walked closer, bent over, and blew out one candle after another. "I like you — sometimes. I'm going to tell you a bit of a secret. You see, there are moments when it appears that a witch has some dastardly, masterful plan in place when in truth, she is simply filling the needs of those who come to her."

Sniffling, Max tried to put her words into place. "You want me to believe that this is all just a coincidence?"

"Not at all. Well, maybe the part when you and your wife came asking questions. I never expected you to fall right into my lap, but I was happy to provide all the guidance you needed to get on the right track. That is, to go the way I wanted you to go."

Max thought back to that meeting and his blood chilled. "This was all about getting to Sandra, wasn't it?"

"Oh, dear me, no," she laughed. "That is to say, I have no idea what is behind Isaac Brown's intentions — well, perhaps. But when you and Sandra entered the picture, then well, yes. I knew Isaac Brown's son was in your care, and I hoped that in some way down the road I might be able to use that information to my advantage. You all simply made it easier."

Another thought hit Max and his chilled blood iced over even more. "Are you planning to kill me?"

"You are so shortsighted. I'm telling you these things because I want you to know who are your allies and who are your enemies."

"And you are?"

"An ally, of course. For now. I don't want that boy harmed. If that happened, you and Sandra would be against me. When the time comes that I will call upon Sandra to fulfill her marker to me, I do not want any of those negative feelings. So I truly hope you get your boy back. But I also want you never to forget what I have the power to do. Underestimate me at your peril."

"That sounds nice and pat for you, but none of it helps me get PB."

With a sigh, she turned away and headed to the back door. "You really need to get some sleep. You're usually smarter than this."

"What are you talking about?"

She turned back to him. "If Isaac Brown has taken his boy, and if Isaac Brown is trying to fulfill his ceremony for wealth and power, then it's safe to assume that he will bring his boy to the final ceremony. What kind of loving father doesn't want to show off for his son?"

Max jumped to his feet — and swooned as he grew lightheaded. With a hand against the wall to steady himself, he said, "Three days. That's what you mean. We know the next part of the ceremony is in three days."

"Perhaps your brain is working after all. Glad to see you didn't hit it too hard on the floor. Now, if you're done acting like an ass, you may leave. And don't forget, your wife owes me."

Before Max could say more, she walked into the back room.

He mulled over everything he had heard. Madame Yan still hid her true purpose from him, but perhaps he would simply have to live with that. She had given him a timeframe to find his boy, and that was a little more information than he had before.

A clock near the iguana read 4 am, so Max texted Sandra to see if she was awake.

How can I sleep? She texted back. *Still at the office. J's half-awake too. Come over.*

Max wondered how many more hours the three of them could go before they crashed. At least Drummond did not need sleep. He took a step toward the door but stopped.

Madame Yan had left him alone. To his side, several of her boxes formed an unsteady tower. One box near the middle looked a lot like the one with Sandra's lipstick. Or maybe he only thought it looked that way.

Leaning toward the back room, he strained to hear Madame Yan. He moved closer to the boxes. Like a safecracker sizing up a challenging vault, Max tried to determine how noisy he might be removing the top three boxes, how long he might take sifting through the lipsticks, and how angry Madame Yan might become if she caught him.

No. PB comes first.

Closing his eyes, he shoved down the desire to find that lipstick. His chest burst as he turned away. Sandra would understand. She would have been angry if he had risked everything for that lipstick. She would agree that PB had to come first. She would forgive him for letting this opportunity go.

He wasn't so sure he could forgive himself, though.

Chapter 19

MAX JOLTED AWAKE with his heart pounding and PB on his mind. He had a crick in his neck and his lower-back felt like a lump of cement. It took his brain a few seconds to recognize that he had fallen asleep on the office couch. J had curled up on the area rug that covered Sandra's casting circle.

Sitting up, Max found his wife at her desk working on her laptop. When she saw him, she beamed her sunshine smile and indicated the coffee pot on the sideboard. "It's only about twenty minutes old."

Scratching his stubble, Max moved to the coffee pot like an old man — slow and in pain with each step. Thankfully, Sandra did not pepper him with endless questions. In fact, she had the loving sense to let him caffeinate in peace.

After drinking down half-a-cup and scalding his tongue, he topped off his mug and sauntered over to Sandra's desk. Sitting next to her, he noticed the time. "Eleven in the morning?"

"You came in here, said we had three days to find PB, and plopped down on the couch. Eyes closed and you were out. You were so tired, I didn't want to disturb you."

"But I've lost so many hours. We've got to stay on this."

Sandra put her hand atop his and kissed his cheek. "I've been up working on the case."

"Then you haven't had any sleep, either. You need rest, too."

"That's why I let you sleep. I figured at least one of us needs to be coherent."

Max could not argue with that logic. As long as one of them worked to find PB, then they were moving forward — together. J snorted, and Max thought he might be awake. But he merely rolled to his side and fell back into a deep slumber.

"How did he handle the witch talk?" Max asked.

"Like a pro. Nothing seems to faze that kid."

Max's eyes drifted from J to a large book on witchcraft opened to some of the basic history. "How many of those has he read?"

"That was only the second. The first one I gave him was more of a children's primer. He ripped through that pretty fast. This one's a little more challenging. Plus, it was three in the morning. He was a bit tired."

Pointing to the rug, Max said, "Did you cast the location spell? If you did, I'm guessing it didn't work because you're really burying the lead if you know where PB is."

"It didn't work." Sandra rested her head on his shoulder. "It's possible that Isaac Brown has some kind of ward or charm to prevent me from finding them. Madame Yan could have given him something like that. More likely, I'm too full of anxiety to properly perform the spell. A witch's emotional state can change the nature of a spell, making it easier or more difficult. Because I love PB and I'm obviously upset, it's possible I just can't pull off the spell. Or maybe I suck at this. Maybe I'm fooling myself to think I could become some talented, good witch."

"Stop that." Max lifted her head by the chin and looked straight in her eyes. "You're only talking like that because you are exhausted. You know you're good at this stuff. So what if we can't use the location spell this time — you keep at it. We'll find some other way. We don't give up. Right?"

"Then I'm going to need another cup of coffee."

Max swiped her mug off the desk and refilled it for her. The muscles in his back had loosened a little, and his mind had found some focus. When he handed over the mug and sat next to her again, he noticed the article on her laptop — an in-depth look at tragedy groups.

"I take it when the spell didn't work, you chose a different avenue."

Sipping her coffee with grateful pleasure, she said, "This is from one of my darkweb witch forums. I think I found something that might help."

Skimming over the article, Max discovered further proof that Madame Yan's involvement in all of this was no accident. Diagrams showed the key parts of any ceremony such a group would need to perform — the rest of what the group did was ritual and window-dressing. Other charts showed the phases of the moon and when the ceremonies would be most effective considering they had to occur over the course of nine days total.

Cradling the hot coffee in her hands, Sandra said, "These tragedy groups are actually an offshoot of some long-gone Christian sects."

"What I saw out there did not look like anything to do with Christianity."

"Not surprising. Every religious group has offshoots that focus more on magic or wish fulfillment, and Christianity has quite a few. When you add in the way Christianity actively courted the pagan groups throughout history, going so far as to incorporate pagan holidays and practices into Christian doctrine, it's not surprising that something like these tragedy groups were born. We're talking about hundreds and hundreds, if not a thousand years ago. What Isaac Brown is involved with now only bears the same name."

"Why are you telling me this?"

"For one, this is how you always tell us everything — you give us the full picture, the full history. For another, I'm your wife — be nice to me. I'm very tired."

Max chuckled. "Sorry."

"I'll cut to the end, for your sake. It's like this — there's a pattern to these three ceremonies. Broad to narrow. The first ceremony was held at a place of broad tragedy."

"Odd Fellow's Cemetery — where over ten thousand slaves are buried."

"Exactly. The second ceremony narrows it down to a large but more personal tragedy — the Lawson family massacre. Finally, it comes down to an individual. Isaac Brown is trying to build a legacy for PB, and he'll have to spill blood at the site of a singular tragedy to get what he wants."

"Hold on." Now that he had rested, Max's brain fired off. "I thought this group was doing the ceremonies so that they would all benefit from wealth and power. But you're talking about narrowing down to an individual with a singular tragedy at the core of the ceremony. Are you saying that Isaac Brown is duping everybody in his group? That he's doing all of this for his own benefit? He's the individual to gain wealth and power off the singular tragedy?"

"And PB. But I don't think the group is being duped. I suspect they all know and over the years have taken turns so that each one of them gets the benefit. Because of the moon phase requirements and the need for specific types of tragedies, the spell can only be cast once every three years."

Max tapped his chin. "Sure. That's why Brown had to wait all these years. Other people with seniority got to go before him. Only now does he get the chance."

"That's what I'm thinking."

"During that time waiting, they must have lost the spell — maybe the previous Soro died before telling anybody."

"And that's why Brown had to deal with Madame Yan."

Stepping behind Sandra, Max kissed the top of her head. "You've done a great job. This is big."

"I don't see how. It's interesting but doesn't really help. From Madame Yan, we know when this next ceremony is going to happen but not where. There are probably millions of singular tragedies all over the state. At least a few hundred thousand right here within a few miles radius of Winston-Salem. How are we to figure out where the Soro Group is going to be next?"

Max jabbed his finger toward the laptop. "Right there. You found all this information about tragedy groups on authentic witch sites. I found my information directly from Madame Yan. We also know that Madame Yan instructed Isaac Brown in what he's doing. Which means that some part of all this bull ceremony he's performing must be real witchcraft; otherwise, the spell wouldn't work."

Sandra straightened in her chair. "If we find what part of the ceremony is real, then you're thinking that will narrow down the places it could be performed."

"All those diagrams about phases of the moon suggest being able to see the moon, so I'm guessing we're not going to be in a cave, for example."

"That's still going to leave us a lot of possibilities."

"We've got three days, and we have to find an answer. It's better than nothing."

J stretched his arms into the air as he woke. Posting up on his elbow, he scanned the office as if trying to remember where he had fallen asleep. A smile crossed his lips as he looked toward Sandra and Max, but his attention then drifted onto the bookcase. Max followed his gaze and found Drummond entering the office.

Once Drummond fully exited the bookcase, he clapped his hands together. "With a little help from my doll, Miss 1800s, I found PB."

Everybody jumped to their feet. Max said, "That's great. Where is he?"

"With his dad in Lexington."

"Lexington?"

"According to Miss 1800s, the two have been sitting at a BBQ joint since the place opened for the day. Seems to me, Isaac Brown is waiting for you to show up."

Chapter 20

NO MATTER HOW TIRED any of the Porter Agency members felt, nobody would agree to stay back. Max, Sandra, J, and Drummond all headed out to the aptly titled restaurant *Lexington BBQ*. It was a large white building right off a curve of Route 64. The restaurant displayed its name in bold, black lettering across the white walls facing the highway. Many considered it to be the best BBQ in all of North Carolina, it had won numerous awards attesting to this, and Max's taste buds agreed. He had indulged at the establishment several times and never once had a bad experience.

He hoped that would hold true this time — even if they never ate a bite.

When they entered, the lunch crowd packed every seat and several people waited in line for their chance to eat. Waitresses old and young hustled plates of chopped BBQ, BBQ sandwiches, plates piled with loose BBQ, and French fries out to hungry customers. The aroma whetted Max's appetite, and he wished he was simply taking Sandra and the boys out for a delicious afternoon meal.

He stepped to the front of the line. "Excuse me."

"Just wait your turn, hon," a cheery, older waitress with tight curly hair said as she hurried by carrying a plate in one hand and two plates — one on the arm — on the other.

"Our friend is already here. He came in with his son."

The waitress nodded. "Oh, they're in the back. Those two are quite the charmers."

"Sure," Drummond said as he floated on the ceiling to avoid passing through the congestion. "He's real charming for a cult leader who likes to murder people."

Max led the way and Sandra and J followed. The restaurant had hard tile floors and several wooden tables shoved too close together. Narrow booths lined against one wall, and every space was filled with customers and food. The music of dishes and utensils blended with the clashing clatter of overlapping conversations. It was like walking into somebody's kitchen that had been expanded into an entire building filled with strangers.

In the back room, Max found Isaac Brown and PB at a group of three tables pushed together. PB stared straight ahead, and Max's heart dropped. He wanted to rush over and hug the boy, but he could barely get eye contact.

Isaac had clearly tried to buy PB's affection. The boy wore a new shirt — silk, black, with white buttons down — and he had a gold chain with a pendant that matched the symbol on the back of Isaac's purple, ceremonial robe. But even without the fancy shirt, Max suspected PB would be enthralled with Isaac. To have his father back after all this time would fill an empty hole in him. The past would wash away and any excuse would be believed because PB wanted to believe. He wanted the chance that this might all be real. Add to that Isaac having enough charisma to win over all his followers, and Max feared he had already lost.

Isaac sat at the head of the table. No robes this time. Instead, he wore a stylish business suit like a well-off man securing a loan from a bank. He stood when he saw Max.

"There you are. I was worried you wouldn't show."

As they filed in, Drummond continued to float overhead. J could not stop peeking up at the ghost but neither PB nor Isaac seemed to notice.

Max said, "You could've called. Then you wouldn't have had to worry."

"Where's the fun in that? Besides, Madame Yan promised you would find us and Gene tells me you're a great detective."

Before PB could correct Isaac, Max said, "His name is PB." A grin appeared on PB's face and a warm flush filled Max's body from that slight expression.

Isaac put a firm hand on PB's shoulder and the boy's grin

widened into a full smile. "Of course. My apologies, PB. I can't really expect everything to go back to the way it was. I've been gone for too many important parts of your life. It's going to take some adjustment."

Isaac spoke with a broad smile and a slight tension as if he were picking up his son from an ex-wife who had remarried. But the darkness behind his eyes could not be mistaken. In fact, as the waitress approached to take new orders, a simple glance from Isaac sent her away.

"I know we got off to a rough start," Isaac said. "I'm not exactly what you expected."

"You mean alive?" Max said, and J snickered. But PB stared at J with a darkness mimicking his father.

"I suppose that part was a bit of a shock, too. But the fact is that I am PB's father, and I want him in my life."

Sandra said, "Is that why you kidnapped him?"

Isaac chuckled as if he had received a playful insult from an old friend. With a knowing wink to PB, he said, "It's a good thing we chose to meet them in a public place. No telling what crazy lengths they might have gone to if they thought nobody was watching."

From above, Drummond said, "I'm watching. Just say the word and I'll freeze him. You can grab PB and get out of here."

J looked to Max, perhaps eager to take Drummond up on his offer. Max put out a hand to stay the boy's enthusiasm. "You assaulted my wife and sons and tied them up in the bathroom."

"I was with you," Isaac said.

"Are we really going to parse words?"

Isaac pressed his tongue against his bottom lip as if he considered the question seriously. "I apologize if the men I sent to collect my son acted in an inappropriate manner. But your wife did throw a knife at one of them. They tend to react quite roughly when people threaten them that way."

Sandra said, "If you think —"

Max spoke up to stop Sandra from ranting — no matter how justified. "PB, look at me."

PB lifted his eyes but focused on Isaac. Isaac gave PB a short nod, and then the boy looked at Max.

Hoping his voice did not break as much as his heart, Max said, “Are you okay? You know we’re tough, so whatever he might have threatened could happen to us if you are honest, you ignore that. Tell me straight out — have you been hurt?”

Sandra said, “This must be such a shock. We’re here for you.”

PB lowered his head, but before he could speak, Isaac snapped his fingers. PB’s head shot up. They exchanged a strong look, and PB pulled back his shoulders and held his head up firm. “I’m absolutely fine.”

Drummond said, “That kid is not fine.”

“You see?” Isaac put an arm awkwardly around PB. “He’s doing just fine. He is not my prisoner or my victim. He is and always has been my son. I love him very much, and I have gone through great sacrifice so that he can live a life I’ve only ever dreamed of.”

Max stopped from speaking. He had come to this restaurant expecting that they were going to be dueling with words like swordsman using vocabulary, but he saw now that they were actually playing chess. And Max had flubbed the crucial opening moves.

In the short silence that grew while he thought, Sandra said to PB, “You don’t have to go with this man. He may have picked a public place so we wouldn’t get into a big shouting match, but it goes both ways. Don’t think that you can’t come home with us. He can’t stop that. He gave up his legal rights a long time ago.”

Isaac grinned as if he had expected that move. “From what I’m told, you have yet to finish the whole guardianship process. So I am still the legal guardian of PB. I’m certainly his father. Parental rights go a long way in this state. However, if you think it best to drag PB through the tedious, and oftentimes ugly, process of court, I suppose we’ll have no alternative. Of course, during that time, PB would stay with me, his father. You might succeed at destroying our family or you might not, but at least my son and I will get to spend a small amount of time together before you tear him away."

This would not work. Any straightforward argument would be easily countered — Isaac had prepared for this conversation. He had anticipated what the typical debate points would be and how to answer them. And every time Max and Sandra failed in front of PB, it only pushed the boy closer to his real father.

"That's the problem," Max said. "Isn't it, PB?"

PB's brow tightened as he listened to this new tactic.

"You want your real father. And I'm not that. I'm just a pale imitation. But ask yourself — who was it that brought you food and water when you lived on the streets? Who was it that helped you fight off the bullies? Who was it that brought you the opportunity to earn a living and broadened that to your pal, J? Who was it that welcomed you into his family, that gave you love and warmth and security? When things have been tough between us, I didn't run away. I certainly did not fake my death. I would never do that to you. I know we don't share the same blood, but there's more to a family than just that."

Max put his hand out on the table, palm up. He searched PB's face for any hint that his words had seeped through. But as the words died in the air, he felt them dying within, too. They were not enough. He needed something with more impact.

Sandra must have sensed it, too. She said, "We love you. That's what it comes down to. We're the ones who keep showing up. We're the ones that you know you can count on."

For a hesitant moment, Max thought he saw cracking in PB's wall. He would think back to that moment many times in the future and wonder if he had said something different, if he had spoken at that exact moment, could he have changed the words PB would speak. But before he could formulate the perfect phrase, Isaac Brown once again proved to be several steps ahead.

Isaac said, "PB? Do you have anything to say to them?"

PB made eye contact with Sandra and Max. "I want to thank you for everything you've done for me."

"You don't have to do this," Max said, his heart locking in his chest.

"Especially you. You started taking care of me when I had nothing. You got me off the streets, gave me a home, and even started my education. I know that it wouldn't be possible for me to be sitting here right now without you."

"You're confused. I understand. But this is not —"

"The thing is that this man here is my father. I care about you all, but you're not my family. He is. I'm with my real father now, and that's how it's supposed to be."

Max opened his mouth, but nothing came out beyond a choked sound. His mind blanked.

PB turned toward J. "Sorry to leave you, but more than anybody here, I guess you'd understand. You stick with the Porters. They're good people, and you know it."

Max sat with his mouth agape, and he could feel Sandra and Drummond and J all staring at him. In some distant land, he heard Isaac Brown stand and utter some words about this conversation settling matters. That receding voice tied to a blurred image of Isaac as he tossed a hundred dollar bill on the table and suggested the Porters enjoy their lunch on him. He then muttered something to PB, and father and son left the restaurant.

Max wanted to walk away. He wanted to run. He wanted to scream and howl and punch the walls and shatter glasses against the wall. But all he could allow was to sit.

His emotions, however, refused him the luxury of that small dignity. The loss welled up inside of him filling his chest like a giant balloon that left no room for his lungs to breathe or his heart to beat. The pain flooded tears into his eyes.

It had been possible, if only briefly, that he might be able to contain himself. But then J put a hand on his arm and said, "It's going to be okay."

Max burst into tears.

Chapter 21

ONCE IT BEGAN, Max could not stop it. As his breathing sputtered out in large gasps, tears drenched his face. He pounded the table with his fist, rattling the dishes, and lowered his forehead against the cool wood of the table. His body shuddered repeatedly.

He could feel Sandra's hand on his back and knew she spoke soft words to him, but it all drowned out in the image on loop in his mind — Isaac Brown taking PB. He kept hearing PB's last words — *I'm with my real father now.* A waitress asked if she could help and the quiet, stunned stares of other customers grew heavy on his shoulders. But nothing could stop the pain-wracking sobs erupting from him.

He tried to pull himself together, but he kept seeing the look in PB's eyes — as if Max was never more than a placeholder to the boy. A vacant glare suggesting that all Max had attempted to create between them had been a forgery. He heard PB's cold pronouncement again — *I'm with my real father now.*

J placed his head against Max's arm which served another howling cry through Max's throat. He put his arm around J and held him tight.

"We should leave," Sandra said, and the words actually made it through Max's ears.

He grabbed a napkin and blew his nose. Dabbing at his eyes, he stood and let Sandra lead him out of the restaurant. J followed. Max assumed Drummond floated nearby somewhere.

Nearing the exit, he exhaled a shaking breath and thought he would be okay. Until he saw a family of four trying to enjoy their meals. He wanted to apologize, but the family's little boy stared at Max with cold curiosity. It broke him again.

Time shifted. He lost a few minutes but found himself in the passenger seat of the car with J in the back and Sandra staring at him from the driver's side. "It's not over," she said.

"Of course it is," Max said. "It doesn't matter what we do. All our options are going to lead to the end of this family. It was all just an illusion from the start."

From the back, J said, "You're talking stupid. PB needs us."

"The stupid thing was ever believing PB could think of me like a real father. You saw the way he acted. He was just using us. Never really wanted to try to make it work. And maybe, maybe we could have changed that. Somehow we could have won his love over in the long run, but now — it's too late." Max wiped his sleeves against his eyes. "I'm sorry about all my blubbering. I knew how much I had grown to care about him, at least I thought I did, but when he tossed us away so easily — it felt like something was ripped right out of me."

Sandra said, "That's how you know you're every bit as much a real father to him as that poser. You are far more of a father. You think Isaac Brown would care if PB chose you?"

J said, "The only thing he wants is to win. He don't care nothing about PB."

Max tried to take a cleansing breath but ended up coughing. "It doesn't matter. It wasn't about winning. At least, not for me. But it's over now. In a few days, they'll perform their ceremony and get rich, and PB will never think about us again."

"What are you talking about?" J said shoving his feet against the back of Max's seat. "Where's all that *push on through* talk that you guys always are doing? Why aren't you trying to save PB anymore?"

"Because PB doesn't want to be saved." Max spoke the words harshly enough that J fell back in his seat. Max went on, "I would think, considering the horrible life you lived on the streets, that you would understand some of this reality. Life gets crappy. Lots of times, for just about everybody. The only reason PB latched onto me was because I offered a hand when he needed one. But he doesn't need it anymore. He's got a better offer on the table. I get it, and so should the both of you.

PB is a survivor. We never got to see the real boy. He put up a façade to appease us so that he could survive in a better situation than he was in before. But now, this guy comes along and promises PB tons of money and maybe even some power in life. Why wouldn't that boy go for it? All we have to offer is us."

The surly expression on J's face caused Max to stop. He had not meant to go so far, to be so hard. But J sat forward, and in a calm yet strong voice, he said, "You don't know shit about what you're saying. I lived on those streets same as PB. And I'm smaller than him. You think he got picked on? I got it worse. I spent tons of nights never getting any sleep because I had to worry about getting raped or beat up or taken away by somebody who wants Lord-only-knows what from me. You think you were the first guy to come along and offer to take us away from the streets? Heck, it happened at least once a month. What made you different was that you actually care about us. When PB came to me and said he found somebody — I knew what he meant. We didn't put on some show for you to try and get you to like us. And you didn't try to become our daddy. All you wanted to do was give us a job, let us earn some money, so we can take care of ourselves. All this family stuff started later. If you don't think it meant the world to PB, then you are a giant idiot. PB's not choosing his old dad over you. PB is confused and his heart is being torn in different directions, and he don't know what to do. But you both, you are our real family. At least, I thought you were. Family fights for each other. Seems like you want to roll over and die now. That's not family."

Max did not know what to say. Every response sounded empty to his ears. J crossed his arms and leaned back in the seat. He stared straight ahead with a defiant scowl but did not make eye contact with Max or Sandra.

Drummond poked his head through the side of the car. It would have been comical, but J's words fell heavy inside Max.

"I'd like a word with you," Drummond said. "Outside."

Chapter 22

MAX WALKED OVER TO THE FRONT OF THE CAR and sat on the hood. The metal felt hot through his jeans and more heat radiated off the car, but he didn't want people seeing him speak to empty space next to the car, so he endured. He pulled out his phone and pressed it against his ear — at least, should any of the customers watch him, they'd see a guy talking on his phone. Observing the cars zip by on Route 64, Max waited for Drummond to say his piece.

The ghost flew directly in front. "I had Intended to bring you out here to smack some sense into you."

"J beat you to it."

"I saw. I'll tell you this — that boy gets more appreciation from me every single day."

Max had a whirlpool of emotions spinning inside him — he did not need to worry about whatever Drummond's take on all of this would be. "Anything else?"

"You better watch your attitude. Just because I'm dead and you're my partner doesn't mean I can't set you straight when necessary."

With an impatient tone, Max said, "I was upset, and I haven't had much sleep the last few days. That's all."

Drummond put his hands in his coat pockets and loomed over Max like he intended to interrogate a suspect. "Easy to say, but I witnessed what happened down there. You just think about this — you are only PB's father if you're willing to fight for him."

"I get it," Max said, putting plenty of force behind the words. "Everybody thinks I'm worthless because I have emotions."

"Cut that out. You want to twist words around to make it all look like you're the victim? You do it when that boy is not in trouble."

Max lowered the phone from his ear. "That's just the thing. PB is not in trouble. His father is going to do a horrible thing and PB will benefit from it. I suppose you could argue he's in moral trouble, but he's made his choice."

Practically chewing his lip off, Drummond said, "Don't make me have to become solid enough to smack you. I don't want that kind of pain today. And while you're busy feeling sorry for yourself, you're not listening to me. The boy is in trouble. In fact, Sandra needs to hear this too. Get back in the car."

Moments later, Sandra drove toward their office. Drummond had to share the backseat with J, and Max could see that neither one was noticeably uncomfortable with the arrangement. But Max did not really care about their comfort — good or bad.

"What did you want to say? Why is PB still in danger?"

"While I floated above your meal — which looked mighty delicious, let me tell you — I could feel magic on Isaac Brown."

Sandra said, "I didn't notice anything. Although, I was wrapped up in trying to get PB to leave Isaac. Maybe I missed it."

"It was subtle. It wasn't a ward, and it wasn't an actual spell surrounding him. It was more like the residue of a spell."

As Sandra took the ramp onto 52 North, which led straight into Winston-Salem, Max saw the grim expression come over her. She said, "The spell must be starting to work. They've already succeeded in completing two parts of the overall ceremony. Whatever it's going to do, it's beginning to touch Isaac Brown."

Max said, "What do you mean *whatever it's going to do?* It's supposed to make him rich and powerful."

"That's what he thinks the spell will do," Drummond said, "but he's hardly a master of witchcraft, and he got his information from Madame Yan. Would you trust that woman as the source for your future?"

Sandra said, "Whatever it's doing, it's starting. That's my point."

"My point is that something is off. I could feel it. That magic residue surrounding him — it did not feel like a simple thing. Not like the kind of warm feeling you might get from something that is going to bring good fortune to a person."

J spoke up. "Does that mean PB really is in trouble?"

"It does," Max said. He let his gaze fall upon every person in the car. "I'm sorry for my outburst. Thank you all for helping me stay focused."

Drummond said, "Partner, we all want the same thing. We all are going to try to get that boy back."

"Well, we've got two days to figure it out. So you and Sandra need to work on determining what spell is actually being used. As for me — I've got to figure out where the next ceremony is going to take place."

The scowl had left J's face as he took interest in the conversation. He said, "I might know."

Chapter 23

ACCORDING TO J, the last time PB ever saw his father, he had tracked Isaac to a spot under one of the crossovers of Business 40 — an old highway cutting through Winston-Salem.

"PB had followed his dad," J said, so eager to tell his tale that his previous anger evaporated like boiling water. "This is after he'd already found out about what his dad was involved with, but he didn't tell you this part. He actually followed his dad lots of times. I guess he didn't want to sound all desperate but that's what happened."

"Business 40? That's a long stretch of road," Drummond said. "A lot of overpasses."

"Yeah, but it has to be a place where a tragedy occurred. Right?"

Drummond snapped his fingers at Max. "Kid's right. You should get on that."

Max could not help it — he laughed. After all the emotional tsunamis he'd been through, laughter felt good.

Sandra and Drummond left to learn what they could about the spell that appeared to be surrounding Isaac Brown. Max and J drove off to the Z. Smith Reynolds Library at Wake Forest University. Being at a school reminded him that J should have gone to school that day. He made a quick call, endured a reprimand from the school secretary, and got J off the hook for not showing up to class.

Walking across the university campus, Max said, "This is one of my favorite libraries. It once was two separate buildings and they closed up the alleyway between and turned it into this beautiful open space that we can work in."

"What kind of work?" J asked.

"Researching Business 40. We'll see if we can find any record of a terrible tragedy happening along that route through the city."

"Under one of the crossovers."

"That's right."

"So if we find that, we'll know where to find PB in two days."

"Exactly."

Max did not know what to expect from J. Few boys would look forward to spending their day stuck looking through old books. But once they entered the labyrinth of the library, it became evident that J had found a second home.

His face lit up. His fingers trailed the rows of books in the stacks, and Max even caught him breathing in the aroma of all those pages.

"You really like this?" Max asked.

"This place? It's awesome. All these books and you can go right up and take them. Read what you want. What's not to love about that?"

"I agree entirely. It's just weird to find somebody who feels the way I do."

"Well, I am your son, right?"

Max stumbled forward, caught himself, and squatted level with J. He put his hands on the boy's shoulders and tried to keep his voice from cracking. "You most certainly are."

"Are you going to start crying again?"

Max pulled J in for a hug. "No. Maybe. I don't know. Let's go get your brother back."

Their first step was to get some simple background on the history of the road. The state government website and Wikipedia provided enough basic information on that part.

Essentially, after the towns of Winston and Salem merged into one back in 1913, the area grew fast. By the 1940s, traffic congestion had turned into a major problem. Winston-Salem had become the largest manufacturing hub in North Carolina thanks to R.J. Reynolds Tobacco and Hanes textiles. Lots of roads came into the city, but there was no simple way to cross from one side to the other.

"Look here," Max said, finding it strange to have somebody hear him talking to his books. Especially somebody who might respond.

J checked out the part Max had indicated. "So from 1940 to 1954, everyone just lived with the problem?"

"Looks like it." Indeed, only in 1954 did the city find the money to start constructing the East-West Expressway. Two years later, the Federal Aid Highway Act was passed and when Winston-Salem took its share of that money, they decided to connect the East-West Expressway with the new Interstate 40. When finished it became the first completed highway in North Carolina.

Since 1958, little had changed despite rising safety standards and better construction methods. In fact, Max and J learned about the infamous Hawthorne Curve. This S-curve overpass of Hawthorne Road became known for the numerous wrecks and deaths it had caused. Especially because the road's tight design was rumored to have been ordered by Mayor Marshall Kurfees in an effort to help out his business pals from being damaged by the original path. Mayor Kurfees denied the corruption charge to his deathbed but that never stopped the rumors.

"Is that tragedy enough?" J asked.

"Not even close. Plus, we're looking for a singular, individual tragedy. This was multiple times with different people."

Recently, the main section of the highway running through the city was closed and cut into pieces as they attempted to finally fix the traffic flow for the modern era. Once completed, the road would no longer be known as Business 40. A website contest for a new name had been conducted and the Salem Parkway would open fairly soon.

Max jotted down some notes. From the corner of his eye, he caught J watching closely. Swallowing hard, Max had to hold back from beaming pride at J's interest.

"Okay, now what?" J said. "How does any of this get us

closer to finding where PB is going to be?"

"When you research, it sometimes takes slow and strange turns. You learn to go with it, but you have to remember why you started in the first place. You said it yourself — we're searching for a tragic event. But we could have wasted hours looking in the wrong place or at the wrong time period. By getting this information, we know what years the highway existed, and that gives us a timeframe to focus on. Now we get to do the fun research."

J rubbed his hands together. "Cool. What's that?"

"The two best places we can look are newspapers from that time and old public police records. If there was a tragic murder or a suicide or any kind of weird death where the highway went under one of the old roads, it should have made it into one or both of those publications."

"Can I look at the police records?"

Max chuckled. "You bet. Those are really neat. You'll find all kinds of bizarre arrests in there."

Although the scope of their search had narrowed some, it was still quite wide. Construction began in 1954 and Isaac's "death" would have been around 2011. Fifty-seven years of police records and newspaper articles. Max showed J how to run some computer searches of the archives but made sure to impress upon the boy that they might fail to find what they're looking for with ease. In the end, they both had to go through numerous years of records — three hours' worth.

At one point, Max went to the restroom, and when he returned, J had disappeared. Max's heart immediately pounded in his chest. But a breath later, he spotted J talking to a librarian. She helped him print out some records off microfiche. He raced back to Max with the warm paper to show him.

"I think I found it. Look, look."

Max read over the police report. In 1982, a man identified as Timothy Newitz had been found in a pool of blood under the Cherry Street overpass. An officer's note in the report referred to *unusual circumstances*. Max's blood warmed. "I think you're right."

"I know it's not much, but it's better than nothing, right?"

"The fact that the police are being coy about what they found suggests it might've been a lot worse than simply a body. That means somebody might've written about it in the newspapers. Thanks to you, we know exactly what day to look at — June 15, 1982. Let's get to work."

Within a few minutes, they confirmed J's discovery. In a little article buried on the eighth page of the Winston-Salem Journal, a reporter described the strange situation of Timothy Newitz. He had been found under the Cherry Street Bridge in what looked to be a suicide. However, the blood beneath him had been drawn into a circle and several disturbing symbols had been formed with the blood as well. The reporter had been unable to identify the language the symbols came from nor why Mr. Newitz would cut open his wrists while also hanging himself. The only thing missing that would have given Max a one hundred percent certainty was a photograph.

Unable to stop, he reached over and hugged J once more. "You did it. This has got to be the place. When we get PB back, it's going to be because of you."

J tried to hide his smile. "Cool. Now what do we do?"

Max sat back and sighed. He hated to kill the moment but saw no point in hiding the truth. "Now, we have to do the worst part of this job. We wait."

Chapter 24

DINNER WAS A QUIET AFFAIR. Max, Sandra, and J ate pasta while each managed surreptitious looks at the empty chair where PB should have been. After dinner and clean up, J sequestered himself in his bedroom with a book — a basic history of Winston-Salem that he had checked out of the library. Max and Sandra exchanged what they had learned. Well, Max did — Sandra absorbed it all, but when her turn came, she only said that she neared an answer yet needed more time before she could share it.

"Tomorrow," she said. "I have to verify a few things."

"Can't you at least tell me what you think is happening? What is the spell all about?"

"If I tell you, it's going to spin your thoughts off in a million directions and you won't be able to do your job properly."

Max tossed his arms in the air. "Everything you just said is going to spin my thoughts off in a million directions."

With a comforting hug, she rested her forehead against his. "Trust me."

And that was it. The rest of the night continued much like dinner — quiet, reflective, marked with bouts of sadness as one of them thought of PB.

Despite J's protests, Sandra took him to school the following morning. Max promised he would miss out on nothing — they still had to get through the entire day and wait until midnight the following day before anything would happen.

Max could sympathize, though. The last thirty-plus hours had been filled with a strange ceremony, a kidnapping, an all-night effort to find PB, a tense lunch meeting, Max's emotional breakdown, and the many hours of research that followed. Life had been barreling down like a runaway train, and suddenly, everything halted. There was nothing more for J or Max to do until the ceremony began.

"How am I going to focus on school?" J said.

Though Max and Sandra both knew it would be hard, J's day would be better spent filled with an education. After dropping the boy off, Sandra planned to follow up on her mysterious idea of what the spell Brown used actually would do. Which left Max alone in the house. Alone with nothing to occupy his mind.

Except he had one more job — call his mother. She needed to know that PB would not be coming in, but he could not tell her the reason. He settled on the simplest explanation — PB was sick. Normally, Max would not dare use such a lame excuse, especially because his mother would insist on coming over to nurse the poor boy, but he had no such fears this time. Mrs. Porter would not break her self-imposed exile. Not yet. She would think it served Max and Sandra right that they had to take care of a sick child without her knowledgeable help.

The call went about as well as Max could have expected. She kept the conversation short — thankfully — but still managed to throw in a few backhanded compliments and passive-aggressive comments. With that task completed, Max returned to having nothing to do but wait.

About an hour later, Drummond slipped through the walls into the living room. "I know that look. You're not having very good thoughts."

"What are you doing here?"

"Going through the same thing as you. Killing time. Waiting for this ceremony is like sitting through a long stakeout but taking out all the fun of actually having something to watch."

Max stretched his arms. "You got that right."

Hovering over the chair opposite Max, Drummond pushed back his hat and puffed his cheeks as he gazed around the room. "Small place like this gets awfully depressing when it's empty."

"And here I was worried you were going to try and cheer me up."

"Sorry. Didn't realize you needed cheering. What's the matter? Besides the obvious."

Max's chest felt the weight of all his thoughts. He had spent so many hours contemplating the very thing Drummond wanted to discuss. Max wanted to discuss it, too. But at the same time, the thought of putting into words the ideas spinning tornadoes in his head exhausted him as much as the act of talking about it.

Drummond said, "You just going to sit there? We've got a lot of hours to get through before the ceremony. You might as well say something."

"Okay, okay, enough. I'll talk if it will stop you from rambling."

"No pressure. If you want to talk, that's fine."

Max was tempted to give Drummond a taste of Sandra's hand on the hip routine but now that he stood on the edge of speaking his mind, he could feel the words bubbling up his throat.

"Do you think I'm being selfish? I mean it. All of this that we're going through is to get PB away from his father. It's all to bring him back to this family, so I can play at the role of father. But that's for me. Doesn't PB have a right to be with his actual father? Especially when the result is going to be great wealth for him. Why shouldn't that boy enjoy money for a change?"

"For starters, it's blood money." Drummond drifted into the center of the room as he spoke. "But the actual problem is that you're looking at everything wrong. PB doesn't need his real father. Nobody gives a crap who slept with who to create who. What PB needs — what he wants deep inside — is a *true* father. That's what any kid wants."

"A true father?"

"Knock off that skeptical tone. I know what I'm talking about. My father wasn't around. I know exactly what I needed. A true father — somebody I could count on. Somebody who when he says *I'll be there to pick you up at twelve,* you know what happens at twelve? He's there. Somebody who's going to teach all the stupid stuff — how to throw a ball, how to mow a lawn, how to tie a tie. But also somebody who's going to show you how to treat another right. Teach that love and sex aren't the same thing. There's a reason people want to fall in love and spend their lives with one person, and it has nothing to do with how gorgeous the person looks or how hot they get your blood boiling. Whether we want to admit it or not, we all want a father who will set down the law when it needs to be set down. Somebody who's not afraid to show us when we're wrong as well as praise us when we're right."

Max watched Drummond and could not find the words to respond. Not only was the ghost correct, but he scared Max with his openness. If ever Max needed to know what dumbfounded felt like, he had experienced it right then.

"Why're we talking about this?" Drummond said, floating over to look out the window. With his back to Max, he continued, "We should focus on contingencies. You and I both know nothing will go the way we plan. Never does. We need some back up ideas."

Welcoming the change of subject, Max said, "Sandra's working on finding out what the spell is. That should give us some direction to go in for our counter-moves."

"That'll help. But I'm not sure it'll be enough."

Max scooted to the edge of the couch. "You got something in mind?"

"I don't know if it's time." Drummond turned back to face Max. "But I don't think I've ever seen you like this. The way you reacted at the restaurant, the all-nighter you pulled, the risks you're taking — you've done a lot of it before but there's a desperate passion in the way you've been acting." He leaned close enough that Max could feel the cold coming off of him. "If we botch this up, we'll never see that boy again."

"I can't tell if you're trying to instill me with confidence or scare the hell out of me."

Backing up, Drummond readjusted his hat. "He told me that I'd know when the time came, and I'm calling it — now is the time. Get in your car. We've got a bit of a drive ahead of us."

"What? Who told you?"

"I'll explain on the way."

"Explain what? Where are we going?"

"To dig up some treasure."

Chapter 25

MAX BROUGHT UP A MAP ON HIS PHONE, and Drummond guided him to a point far south near the town of Mocksville. The map made it clear — there was nothing out there but acres of woods. Drummond insisted he remembered the location correctly, and so Max drove on. At worst, the long trip would eat up many hours of the day.

"In the years before I died," Drummond said, "after I left the police department, I had my own little team who would help me with my cases. Especially those involving ghosts and witchcraft. I never was a researcher like you."

"Shocker."

"I had an old friend named Leroy Parker. He was a colored fellow — sorry, black fellow — and he lived in a small shack of a house out in the middle of the woods we're heading towards. He was a cantankerous old bastard but smart as a whip. Had quite a collection of books on witchcraft. Sandra would've been envious. Whenever I came upon the kinds of things that send you and your wife into researching, I relied on him."

As Max headed on Route 64 and crossed the Yadkin River, he started to think that perhaps he should have stayed home. Traipsing through the woods to find the remains of a house belonging to a man obsessed with witchcraft did not sound like a smart idea. Then again, considering the world Max lived in, he had to ask, "This Leroy Parker — he's not still alive, is he?"

"Died a long time ago. Moved on, too."

"So what are we going out there to find?"

Drummond turned his head away from Max and stared out the window. "Last case I ever had with Leroy, I think he knew he would be dying soon. He told me that he had buried a trunk near his house — right outside his chimney. Said that I should never dig it up unless everything is falling apart and I had no other option."

"I know things are bad, but they're not that bad."

"He also told me that there may come a day when I see that I don't ever need what's in that trunk, that I want to give it to somebody else. He said I'd know when the time was right. That's why we're going out today. That's why I'm giving this trunk to you."

"Hold on a second. With all we've been through, you've never once thought we might need it before now?"

"He said not unless I had no other option. There always was another option. Maybe I'm wrong about now, maybe we have a better way out, but I hate to see that kid get caught up in everything. I want to make sure he's got every chance to get through this."

"Okay — so what's in the trunk?"

Drummond shrugged. "Leroy never told me. But you better believe it's going to be powerful."

The further away from Winston-Salem they traveled, the thicker the trees grew. All around them became forest. Occasional areas had been cut clear for housing but long swaths were darkened in the shadows of trees. Max's nerves felt the darkening as well.

Drummond sighed as they crossed an intersection with an ancient gas station on one side and an empty lot on the other. "This area was all forest back when I was alive. Look at it now. I don't know which is scarier — the dark woods or the unending sprawl."

"The dark woods," Max said as they re-entered a tree-filled section. "Definitely, the dark woods."

A short time later, Drummond pointed to the side of the road. "Up there."

Max slowed and pulled over onto the grass. He parked the car before a dirt path that led into the woods.

"Is that a road?" he asked.

"Leroy valued his privacy more than anything. Back in my

day, you could attempt to get a Packard or a Plymouth U up that narrow path, and as long as it didn't rain and turn everything to mud, you might even succeed. But I learned fast, it was better to park out here and hoof it in."

Max turned off the car. From the backseat, he grabbed a shovel and an empty duffel bag. "Then I guess I'm hoofing it."

Hiking through the woods brought to mind all the fairytales about the dangers found deep in the forest. This wasn't the first time Max had followed Drummond into a darkened wood. It probably wouldn't be the last. But even with daylight poking through the leaves and dappling the ground with spots of warmth, even then, Max felt an eerie chill enveloping him. Most humans had left the woods a long time ago because, like the dark itself, the trees created an unknown, mysterious, and unseen otherness.

A few feet ahead, Drummond floated through the trees as he led the way. Over his shoulder, he said, "Don't stray. A lot of bad things have happened out here."

"Great. That makes me feel better."

Off to the left, dry leaves rustled and dead branches snapped as some animal skittered away. The wind picked up for a moment, swishing through the tree branches, to create a sound like rain. The only thing missing was the mournful howl of a lone wolf.

When they reached the house — what remained of it — Drummond stopped several feet from what would have been the front door. Charred wood no more than ankle-high formed a small rectangle that outlined where the dwelling had once stood. The brick chimney had endured, though the top had crumbled down over the years leaving a reddish ruin about nine feet high.

It had been eighty years since Drummond last saw the place, and Max could tell the experience hurt. An oak tree had grown near the middle of the house, and with so many decades passing undisturbed, it reached high up with a thick, sturdy trunk.

"Well look at that," Drummond said. But he was not

remarking on the tree. He pointed to the left of the oak where Max spotted half of a bookshelf leaning precariously to the side. Only three rusted coffee cans kept the thing standing. Only two books remained on its shelves.

"Can we go in?" Max asked. Not that there was a real *inside* — just a hint of dark lines in the ground where walls once had been.

Drummond nodded. "Be careful what you touch, though."

While Max could have walked straight to the bookshelf, he approached through the front door area. Walking around the oak, he noticed three wards carved into the brick of the chimney. One he recognized as a simple warning against magic. The other two he did not know, but clearly they were not ghost wards as Drummond followed behind with ease.

Rubble on the ground, bits of old shattered glass, shards of wood — it formed a floor, of sorts, that crunched and crackled under every step. Covered in dust, the bookshelf looked so fragile that Max feared moving either book. No need, it turned out — the first was a history of the Underground Railroad in North Carolina and the second was a book of spells for influencing animals. However, even from his limited angle, Max could see that all of the pages were missing.

He scanned the tattered floor. "I thought you said Leroy Parker collected all kinds of witchcraft books. Where are they?"

"Probably sitting on the shelves of many of the witches we know. The moment he died, I have no doubt that individual witches and maybe even a coven trekked down this way to scavenge what they could. That's why Leroy buried the treasure he wanted me to have. He knew anything left in the open was going to be taken." Drummond made a circle of the perimeter, his face always gazing outward. "You better get digging."

Max paused. "You see something?"

"I see more than one something. Hurry up."

Armed with his shovel, Max jogged over to the dilapidated chimney. "Where in front of the chimney should I dig exactly?"

As Drummond came around again, he pointed to a specific spot in the dirt. "Whatever's down there, I can see it glowing."

"Either Leroy put a spell around it —"

"Or it's magic. But we won't ever find out if you keep talking instead of working."

Max got digging. He did not like the nerves in Drummond's voice. Every time the wind blew through the trees and his skin chilled, he thought that certainly this would be an attack by a ghost. But the attack did not come. Whatever haunted these woods, whatever put Drummond on edge, it had yet to make its move. Max continued digging.

The dense Carolina clay made the work difficult and slow. In only a few minutes, sweat drenched Max's shirt. Thankfully, Leroy Parker buried the trunk when he was an old man — he had not wanted to dig too deep, either.

Max hit the top of the trunk within ten minutes and proceeded to widen the hole over the next ten. Sweaty and aching, he managed to get around the edges enough to find the latch.

The trunk looked like an old army issue — flat top, olive green, big enough to fit a man's gear and little else. Using the blade of the shovel, Max smashed open the latch — buried for eighty years, it more or less disintegrated upon impact.

Drummond flew up behind. "Open it up, grab what's inside, let's get out of here."

Half-expecting a blinding magical light to shine forth, Max gently lifted the lid. Inside, the trunk was nearly empty. All except for a single small book. It fit in the palm of his hand and reminded Max of a child's practice notebook — a plaything that did not meet any practical purpose.

But when he opened the book he found each of the small pages held a single hand-drawn symbol. The author of these designs wrote in calligraphy. Each page bore one symbol — nothing more. No explanations.

"Come on," Drummond said.

"Just a second."

"When I told you a lot of bad things happened here, perhaps I wasn't clear enough. A lot of bad things happened here because of me. These woods are filled with some mighty angry ghosts, and that anger is directed towards two people — Leroy Parker who's moved on and me. Can we please get going?"

Clasping the book in his right hand, Max stood. "Sorry."

As they headed away from the house, Drummond stopped and turned around. "That's not good."

Max could feel the chill on his back, and this time, he knew it was no simple breeze against his sweat. He heard an animalistic grunt, and he had the strange thought that perhaps a bear had followed them. But when he turned around, he saw a bear of a man hulking forward. Muscular and bald, a crude binding spell had been carved across his forehead. The man glowed with the same pale ghostly light as Drummond.

Max stumbled back and fell to the ground. He only ever saw Drummond. How could he be seeing another ghost?

Chapter 26

SHARP PEBBLES CUT INTO MAX'S HANDS as he stared up at this monstrous ghost. Drummond lunged forward, throwing a right cross against the man's jaw. He followed with a left, but the man caught Drummond's arm and whipped him around. Max watched the pale figures tussle, his mind locked upon a single thought — *how can I see this other ghost?*

Perhaps it was some residual effect from all the time he had spent cursed by Mother Hope. Perhaps one of the wards on Leroy Parker's chimney forced a ghost to be visible in the surrounding area. Or perhaps his ability to see Drummond had begun to grow. All of those answers seemed possible yet none of them felt right.

The man popped Drummond twice in the gut, but Drummond countered with an uppercut that caught the man off-guard. "Now look McMurtry, we've both been dead a long time. There's no need to keep holding this grudge."

McMurtry charged forward angry as a bull. "You cursed me."

"You were killing people."

"It was the witch's fault. She made me."

"What can I say? You shouldn't play with witches. You end up cursed."

They traded blows. Drummond appeared to have things well in hand — he took a couple of hard hits, yet Max had seen him fight many times before. He could handle McMurtry. But then Max noticed the pale glows in the distance.

Rushing to his feet, he said, "We've got more company."

Drummond shoved McMurtry hard and managed a quick look through the trees. He peeked back, and his face told Max everything.

"More of your old friends?" Max said.

Returning his focus to McMurtry, Drummond said, "Get into Leroy's house. He was a paranoid old man. Kept salt everywhere."

Hurtling over a fallen log, Max jumped into the detritus of Leroy's floor. He searched around the base of the chimney and even stuck his hand up the fireplace flue. Nothing. His eyes immediately rested on the bookshelf.

"Stay down, McMurtry." Drummond stood over the large bald man — both hovering three feet in the air. McMurtry appeared to have lost his will to fight.

"Remember me?" A shrill voice called as one of the distant pale figures floated forward.

The woman wore a dressing gown from the early-1900s. She carried a long-handled axe on her shoulder and an empty, soulless glaze in her eye.

Tipping his hat as if passing a charming lady on a Sunday stroll, Drummond said, "Ms. Walker. I wish I could say it was a pleasure to see you again, but I had hoped our paths would never cross once more."

She opened her mouth to reveal jagged teeth. "And here I have been, trying so hard to cut my tether so that I could visit you and have a little vengeance, er, visit."

"I didn't kill you, and I didn't curse you. You've got a coven of witches to thank for that."

With a harsh scowl, she said, "But you told those witches where to find me. You set them loose, and you knew what they would do." He tried to answer, but she let out a cackling scream, and launched after Drummond, axe held high.

The wind had died, yet Max felt increasing cold pressing against his back. His breathing shallowed. He continued to watch Drummond and Ms. Walker but he did not process what he saw.

His mind focused on whatever stood behind him. He listened closely — what could he expect to hear? Ghosts did not breathe and unless they were touching the corporeal world, they would make little to no sound. Unless they wanted to be heard. Unless they spoke.

A wet, mucous-filled laugh — low and guttural — assaulted Max's ears. With a shriek, he whipped around. He stumbled back but managed to stay standing. The ghost — a hunched elderly man, gaunt and toothless — floated partially in the chimney.

Max rushed over to the old bookshelf. If any of Leroy Parker's salt remained, it had to be there. Logic suggested it would be in one of the rusting coffee cans.

Despite the shaking in his hands, Max swept aside the rotting wood of the bookshelf. It clattered to the ground, sending puffs of dust into the air. Coughing, he peered down. All three cans had salt. He snatched up one and quickly poured a circle around himself.

The decrepit ghost in the chimney cackled away, but he did not approach. Feeling slightly more secure, Max turned his attention to Drummond.

The ghost had disarmed Ms. Walker and held the axe above his head. She squawked and disappeared into the darkness of the woods. As she vanished, so did the axe.

With less bravado and more anger, Drummond pointed at all the ghosts watching from a distance. "Anybody else?"

As he swished a circle around the entire area, Max noticed McMurtry regaining his confidence. The big man rolled his muscular shoulders and rocked his head from side to side. By the time Drummond returned, McMurtry cracked his knuckles and growled. Drummond stopped. He shook his head. "Are we really going to do this again?"

With a roar, McMurtry blazed forward. He got under Drummond's punch and tackled him to the ground. Max wanted to help, but he had no play. One step out of that salt circle and old chimney man would be on him.

Max's pant pocket felt warm. For a second, he feared he may have lost his bladder control, but patting his leg, he discovered heat yet nothing wet. He reached into his pocket and pulled out Leroy Parker's little book. It had a soft glow like a nightlight and the warmth brought all the comfort of a favorite blanket on a winter evening.

Ignoring the shaking of his hands, Max opened the book with one finger. The first page had a gentle, blue sheen. The symbol on it had a curved top and scraggly bottom, and it hit Max that it resembled the shape of old chimney man. With that thought, the page slipped out of the book.

Max held this small piece of paper between his thumb and finger — campfire warm yet still radiating blue. Max looked over at the old ghost. The pale figure stared back, but his laughter had stopped.

Working entirely on instinct, Max stepped out of the salt circle. As he lifted the paper, the old ghost hissed. In a flash like a magician's trick, the paper burned bright for a second until nothing remained but a puff of smoke. The same went for old chimney ghost. Just a puff of smoke.

The glow of the book ceased as did Its warmth. Max looked over at Drummond and saw his partner holding empty space in a headlock. He looked all around the woods — the ghosts were gone from Max's sight.

Drummond said, "I can't hold this guy forever. If you're going to make a run for the car, go now."

As the words hit with an electric jolt, Max jumped into action. He sprinted through the woods, leaping over rocks and logs while branches whipped by. He heard Drummond yell and McMurtry cry out.

Somewhere behind him, Drummond said, "Keep going. Keep going."

Though Max could not see them anymore, he imagined all the ghosts surrounding him as if he stood in a cemetery. He kept his eyes focused ahead for fear of tripping should he dare look in any other direction. But there had been so many ghosts. They had to be following. Had to be watching. Had to be closing in.

He burst through the tree line and tumbled onto the dirt pathway. Squinting against the bright afternoon sun, he scrambled to his feet and fumbled out his keys. Hustling to the car, he glanced back to see Drummond racing up behind. Max smiled.

"Don't stand there like an idiot. Get the car going," Drummond said.

Breaking from the tree line behind Drummond, McMurtry barreled forward.

With all the grace of a cow on a sheet of ice, Max bumbled his way into the driver seat. He dropped his keys, flailed about for them, managed to get them in the lock, and turned over the car. Drummond passed through the door.

A loud thump on the roof. Max looked up to see a dent appear above him.

"Are you going to sit there and watch McMurtry rip your car to shreds or can we go?" Drummond asked.

"Won't they just hold on?"

"Do you not remember anything about ghosts? The tether?"

Max slammed on the gas and struggled to maintain control as they fishtailed their way off the grass and onto the asphalt. The thumping stopped as Max quickly put half a mile between them and the woods. Glancing behind, Drummond said, "Well, that didn't go as I had planned. Hope it was worth it."

"Considering that your friend's little book saved my life, I'm thinking it was good."

"What about me? Didn't I save your life, too?"

Max checked the dashboard clock. "You might have to save my life again. Sandra will want to kill me when I call to tell her she has to go pick up J. I'm never going to get back in time."

Drummond chuckled. "Don't worry. When she sees Leroy's book, I think all will be forgiven."

Max drove on at a more sensible speed. He hoped Drummond was right — not just about Sandra, but that Leroy's book might help them get PB back safely.

Chapter 27

MAX PICKED UP A PIZZA on his way back, and when he made it home, Sandra and J pounced on the food. He had been prepared for disappointment or anger, but instead, Sandra smiled at him. "When it was just you and me, it was easy to get bent out of shape if things didn't go one way or the other. But now — this life doesn't work unless we're willing to bend a little."

Later that evening, Max shared with Sandra the day's experiences. As expected, she took great interest in Leroy Parker's book. When Max went to bed that night, Sandra still poured over each page, trying to find correlating symbols in her various references.

The next morning came fast, but once Max got out of bed, time slowed to a near halt. The world knew that he needed it to speed up, needed to reach the midnight witching hour, needed to save PB. It must have known. Because the world always found a way to taunt.

Through this interminable slowness, Max prepared breakfast, cajoled J through his morning routine, and drove the boy to school. Although J continued to complain about not being part of PB's rescue and while his fear for his brother was real, he accepted that he would only have limited participation.

"It sucks being young," J said.

Max laughed. "It sucks being old, too."

When he got back home, Max waited for Sandra to take a shower, and the two of them settled in their tiny living room. Like conspirators in some smalltime heist, they sat on the sofa with their heads close to each other looking down at the little book.

"I still haven't figured out how this thing allowed you to see ghosts," Sandra said.

"Only for a short time. It was like the book knew I needed its help."

"And it provided one page for you that stopped this other ghost — the one in the chimney?"

"Afterward, the page burned up."

Thumbing through the remaining pages, she said, "Each symbol is different. Maybe they do different things."

"The one that burned up was shaped a lot like the ghost it got rid of. Is it possible that each page is a symbol for a specific ghost?"

"The resemblance of the symbol to your ghost in the chimney was probably in your head. It's the way our brains work — always trying to find patterns. If each symbol corresponded to a specific ghost, then that would not make this book very useful — unless you were going to try and destroy all those specific ghosts. But you said that this was a gift to Drummond meant to help him. Right?"

"That's what Drummond said. And he gifted the book to me."

"Then we have to assume that it's not as specific as you're suggesting."

Max flipped through all the strange symbols. Some were simple curves with a sharp jagged line at the end, some were complex structures that rivaled any symbols he had seen Sandra use. "One thing's for sure — there are only fourteen more pages in this. Whatever else it does, it won't be doing a lot of it."

"Hopefully, you'll never have to use it again."

Max raised an eyebrow at her.

"What? I said *hopefully*."

Pocketing the book, he scratched his head and rested his back on the sofa. "What did you find out about the spell Isaac Brown is casting? You said you needed more time — well, today's the day."

With a guilty wince, she said, "I swear I will give you an

answer before we go out tonight."

"What more can you possibly be waiting for?"

"The phone. One of my contacts is going into her private library to double-check something for me. She will call me, and if it's confirmed or not, I promise I will tell you what I know."

Max grumbled, but he let Sandra have her moment. Perhaps her caution was warranted. Perhaps if he knew whatever she hid, it would send him off in a direction that might not help PB. She knew him so well that he had to trust her judgment on this. But that didn't make it easier to swallow.

Over the course of the day, every time the phone rang, Max watched Sandra expectantly. The call they wanted did not come. He spent time online checking out images of the construction site where they planned to go that night. He worked out strategies for ways to approach Isaac Brown and how to handle various reactions. But it was all busy work. They had already thought through it all numerous times over the last few days.

When three o'clock rolled around, Max had never been so grateful to have to pick up J from school. Simply getting out of the house with a clear task that did not involve ghosts or magic or a kidnapped boy helped to clear his mind.

Unfortunately, it would not last. Not only because of the impending task that evening, but because there was no way Max and Sandra would take J with them. That left one place for J to go. Max drove to his mother's apartment.

Thankfully, J understood. "I kind of figured it out already. If you're making me go to school, you ain't taking me with you tonight."

"It's too dangerous."

"I said I get it. What good would it be if you guys go trying to save PB and I get myself snatched away? Then you're right back where you started." J watched traffic zip by as Max turned into his mother's apartment complex. "I still stand by what I said this morning — being young sucks."

Mrs. Porter opened her door, took one look at Max's face, and shook her head. "I have plans tonight."

"I need you to change them," Max said, attempting a pleading and hopeful expression.

"Oh, sure. I'll just change my whole life because you want it." She bent down and kissed J's forehead. "Go on in. You know where the cookies are."

As J scooted into the apartment, Max noted that his mother did not step back to allow him to enter. "Really?" he said.

"I'm not taking any chances. All I've heard this week is how sick PB's been. You think I want the germs that rubbed off on you rubbing off on me? I'm an old lady. I don't handle getting sick so easily anymore."

"What about J?"

"For him, I'll risk it."

Max swallowed back the slew of comments flooding into his mouth. "We probably won't be back until morning."

"Take the night. Take the whole week. Nobody really cares about what I want."

"Stop it," Max said. The force in his voice shook her. "Let me in. I have to tell you something."

He saw the shift on her face — his tone frightened her. She backed up, let him in, and closed the door. They stood in that small entryway as Max told her a lot of the truth. Not all, of course. She would not want to hear about witches, magic spells, or any of that. But she certainly understood that PB's father had crawled out of the swamp of the past and absconded with the boy.

"Why haven't you called the police?" she asked.

"It's not that simple. He is PB's father. There's no restraining order against him. There's nothing that says what he's doing is wrong. He has every right to take his son. Heck, we're not even officially guardians yet."

"Almost. The final paperwork should be coming through any day."

"But it's not in our hands yet. Calling the police will probably backfire and cause us more harm than good. Worst case, it ruins our chances of being guardians."

Mrs. Porter's face tightened as if she bit into a rotten apple.

"This is nonsense. I know some good lawyers who will be happy to take on the case. Probably won't even charge you. Do it *pro bono.*"

Max stepped closer and took hold of his mother's shoulders. "You're not listening. We are not calling the police and we are not getting a lawyer. Tonight, Sandra and I are going to bring PB back home where he belongs. That's why I need J to spend the night here. And I need you to protect him." He paused — not to let his words sink in but to summon the courage to speak his final thoughts. "This man — PB's father — he's dangerous. And he's not alone. He has people who work for him. If anybody comes to your door, if anybody's out in the parking lot watching you, if anything at all makes you even slightly suspicious, do not wait. Don't dismiss it. Don't doubt yourself. Get J, get in your car, and leave."

"You're scaring me."

"I'm trying to. If the slightest thing happens that sets off your radar, then go. I don't care where. Leave the state, go back to Michigan, drive west until you run out of gas, whatever — just go. I'll call you in the morning, and we'll figure out what to do then."

"This is crazy."

"You're damn right. If all goes as it should tonight, none of that will happen. You'll spend the night here, and we'll pick up J in the morning. We'll have PB with us, and everything will be fine. But if things go bad, can I count on you?"

All of Mrs. Porter's worry vanished. She puffed up her chest, lifted her chin, and stared straight into Max's eyes. "I'm your mother. I'm always here for you."

He hugged her. "I love you."

"The boys are lucky to have you in their life. You're an exceptional father."

"I haven't done anything yet."

She patted his cheek and gazed upon him with pity. "You've done more than you will ever know."

* * * *

Max left for the office. Sitting around his house any longer would have driven him mad, and Sandra had said she would meet him there to prepare for the night. As he walked in, she had her phone to her ear and pointed at it with a big smile.

Relief washed over him. Until that moment, he had not realized how great the tension in his body had become over this single expectation. While she spoke — her end of the call consisted of the occasional *yes, no,* and little more — he fixed a pot of coffee and settled at his desk.

Drummond slipped out of the bookcase. "It's about time you got here. She's been on the phone for almost a half-hour and hasn't said a word worth overhearing."

"I'm sure she's sorry she can't entertain you."

Floating to the middle of the room, Drummond clicked his tongue. "You try being dead for almost a hundred years. Turns out you want every bit of entertainment you can get."

Sandra set the phone down. "Well, then you're in luck. I'm going to entertain you with information about a certain spell we've been trying to figure out."

Max drummed his hands on his desk. "Thank goodness. I'm all ears."

She looked over her notes and pulled together her thoughts. As impatient as Max felt, he knew what it was like to be on the other side of explaining things. He reined in his impatience.

"To start, the spell is real. Strip away all of the Soro Group's nonsense, and at the core is a very real spell." She paused to let that sink in. "It has no official name because it's not a singular spell that a witch can call upon with ease. It's classified as a *pentaid* — literally five spells woven together. That's part of what took me so long. You can weave almost any spells, so the number of combinations possible is ridiculous. That's why there's no name for the spell. Though I suppose a witch that creates a pentaid could name it whatever she wants. The thing is that with so many possible spells involved, it was not easy to identify the ones being used by Brown. I had to go through a lot of old books as well as talk to a lot of old witches. Pentaids are extremely rare, and in this case, the five spells are very old and a few are mostly forgotten."

Drummond said, "Two guesses at the name of the witch behind this mess of a spell."

"That's right — Madame Yan. It's obvious to me that we have underestimated her. We knew she was a witch and have always been cautious with her, but come on — let's admit that we thought of her as a harmless, crazy, old bat living under the ground."

Max propped his feet on the desk. "She definitely played that up with us."

"You've probably already guessed that a spell made up of other spells is quite complex and serves more than one purpose. Basically, Madame Yan is using this Soro Group as a backdoor to try to gain power."

"Like what kind of power?"

"If Isaac Brown succeeds and pulls off this spell, he will get the wealth he seeks, but a huge amount of natural energy will also flow through him for a time — my best guess is that it'll last for about a week. He'll become like a human spellgun."

"And Madame Yan will be the finger on the trigger."

"With that power, she'll destroy the Hulls, Madame Ti, and any other witches who oppose her. When it ends, she'll be on top. If she plays it right, within a week, she will control all of magic in the state. She'll be set up for further growth, too, I'm sure."

Drummond pursed his lips as he coasted in a circle. "If this is such an old and complex spell, why would she entrust it to Isaac Brown? Why should she expect him to be able to pull it off?"

"I wondered the same thing. One of my witch sources told me that it was not uncommon long ago for witches to use a non-witch in this way. Especially back in the *burn 'em at the stake* days. They learned how to package a complex spell into a form that a novice could handle. The novice would have no idea why it worked or how, but as long as they followed the instructions exactly, everything would be fine."

"I take it the *exactly* part didn't always go so well."

"The more complex the spell, the more exact the novice would have to be. One slip up in pronunciation, one mistake when drawing symbols, and bad things often resulted. But for the witch, when things went bad, the novice acted as a buffer between the witch and the spell. It would be difficult for anybody to trace the magic back to her unless that person knew magic — which they would not want to admit. The novice could say anything and would not be believed."

"So this whole thing is just a way to keep Madame Yan's name out of it?"

"Partly. But also, I think she didn't have a choice. Blending these five spells was the difficult part. She must've been working on this for many years. Not only did she have to weave the spells so that they would do the job she wanted, but she also had to have the spell pay off for a tragedy group — otherwise, they would never believe the stuff worked — and then she had to put it all in a package that the tragedy group could actually utilize. I suspect Isaac Brown's Soro Group is not the first she's ever worked with."

Max sat forward. "She's probably been doing this for decades. Each tragedy group she worked with failed, or they succeeded but the part of the spell designed for her benefit failed. It's been a ton of trial and error. Refining it little by little."

"If she had been performing all those spells herself, somebody would have figured out what she was up to. The Hulls, at their height of power, would have shredded her soul. By using the tragedy groups, Madame Yan's experiments read like just another part of a long history of non-witches playing with power they don't understand."

"Except now, she thinks she succeeded."

"From everything I can see with that spell, she may be right."

"Great," Drummond said. "Not only do we have to save the boy, now we have to stop this spell from rewriting the way magic is controlled in the entire state."

Max crossed the room to pour a mug of coffee. His right

hand conducted the rhythm of his thoughts as he walked. "Are we sure we have to stop the spell? Obviously, we have to save PB. But is it a bad thing for Madame Yan to take out Cecily Hull and Madame Ti and a couple of other witches?"

With a gentle but confident tone, Sandra said, "Absolutely. Because I had that thought, too. So, I researched Madame Yan, and you won't like what I've learned." She checked the time before continuing. "Madame Yan has a long and dark history. Nothing like Mother Hope or Grandma Mobley — she did not use magic to extend her life abnormally — but she certainly does like to use magic. She's lived all over the world under numerous aliases. I found three in particular including Madame Court in Czechoslovakia, Madame Vee in South Africa, and Madame Tsung in Japan. In all three cases, she was forced to leave those countries, often late at night before anybody knew she had gone. She's used magic to kill people in horrendous ways. In one case, she boiled a man's brain from the inside."

"Like a microwave?"

"I think so. She's also tortured people, cut them up into small bits for her collections, and in South Africa, she started collecting children — well, their eyeballs. But the key thing is that in every place she's gone, she's always attempted to take control of the area."

Drummond snickered. "Doesn't look like she's too good at it. Maybe we don't have much to worry about."

"A lot of failure only means she's learned what not to do. Don't forget — she's been working at this particular tactic for many years. She's not a clear-minded person. She's erratic and prone to following her whims. If she actually succeeds and is the ruling body of magic here — it will be chaos."

"Well, Doll, there's a bright side — the Porter Agency will have plenty of work."

Max said, "I hate to admit this, but we're probably better off with Cecily Hull. At least she's somewhat sane."

"One last thing," Sandra said as she grabbed a mug of coffee, too. "If Isaac Brown pulls off the spell, it will ultimately consume him. When the energy flow finishes, when the week is up, there won't be anything left of him."

"So?" Drummond said.

"Damn," Max said. "She means that if this spell goes off, PB is going to lose his father. Again."

Sandra said, "It's worse than that. There is a reason you don't see a lot of these pentaid spells. Weaving together five spells of any type is absurdly complicated. When you make them as old and rare as the type Madame Yan is using, it's even worse. The end result is magic that's not really stable — and that's if it's done right. Putting it in the hands of a novice, even one that's spent most of his life practicing for this single spell, is nothing but reckless. The spell will consume Isaac Brown, but it might also consume anyone connected to it when it's initially created."

The coffee in Max's stomach threatened to come back up. "That would mean PB, too."

"I'm afraid so."

Max's phone lit up and the opening chords of AC/DC's *Back in Black* rang out — the alarm Max had set in case he fell asleep. He set his coffee mug down, crossed his arms, and looked up at Drummond. "Sandra and I are in this to the end, but it's not an official case. PB's our boy and there is no way we're backing down. But I can't ask you —"

"Don't you dare finish that sentence, partner. If PB is your son, that makes me Uncle Marshall. Simple as that."

Max walked over to his desk and picked up his coat and keys. His body tingled as if he were a high school student preparing to step out on stage in front of the entire school. They had faced so many horrible things over the years that it surprised him when he still got nervous. But it made him feel good, too. It meant that he had not become jaded, that he still valued his life, that he had people he loved and worried about, that he was as far from the insanity that drove Madame Yan as he could possibly be.

"Okay," he said, opening the office door. "It's time."

Chapter 28

THE SECTION OF CONSTRUCTION THAT CONCERNED MAX was only seven blocks southwest of their office, but they decided to drive anyway. Walking would have used up a lot of energy, and they did not want to be tired before their confrontation began. Plus, Drummond pointed out that once they had PB, they would want to escape fast. So, after gassing up his car, Max and Sandra drove down to 1st Street and spent a short time looking for an available and well-situated parking spot.

Between all of their prep work and driving around, they had managed to eat up plenty of time. With a half hour to go, they approached the construction site one block east of Cherry Street. Turned out getting onto the site was easy. The construction company put up plenty of obstacles, but with such a long swath of road closed off, there were numerous gaps one could sneak through — especially after teenagers started breaking in for fun.

The project reminded Max of images he had seen of the LA waterways — wide and deep ditches, angled at the sides, flat at the bottom, cutting straight through an urban area. The California version had been covered in concrete, and Max would not have been surprised if the same would be done here. But at the moment, it was a lot of Carolina red clay. The angles were steeper here and several of the roads crossing over had been blocked off. A few bridges had been demolished. In the distance, Max saw where they were constructing new on and off ramps. However, the majority of the roads did not exist yet.

"We're lucky it's not raining," he said. "This place would be a mud bath."

As he and Sandra carefully climbed toward the bottom,

Drummond hung at their side. "I think they're definitely here," the ghost said.

Max looked over at Cherry Street. Between the lights of the city and the floodlights set up for the workers, most of the construction site was well-illuminated. Except for Cherry Street. For several feet in front and behind, the bridge remained in the dark. And underneath, where the ceremony would take place, it appeared pitch black.

Max said, "Is that part of the spell?"

"Partially," Sandra said. "You can also see where they knocked out the streetlights and the work lamps."

Drummond said, "Isaac Brown was smart. To do this properly, he needed a night when there would be no work going on. Maybe he has some people on the inside who arranged it this way or maybe he found out that this was going to be a night off, but I'd wager that he picked this specific night for the ceremony and worked the timeline backwards to make sure Walter Klein's death happened on the correct day."

Sandra added, "He'd have to time it with the correct phase of the moon, too."

"Then he's extra-prepared," Max said.

As they reached the bottom, Drummond said, "Don't spend too much time out in the open. They're going to be wrapped up in their ceremony, but a wandering eye could still catch you."

Max took Sandra's hand and they scurried behind a bulldozer. Like soldiers moving in on a fortified position, they dashed from one area of cover to another. Slowly, they progressed forward, and as they closed in on the ceremony, Max could see the cloaked figures of those that had gathered to perform the spell — their images emerging out of the magic-created dark like gothic statues in a fog-covered cemetery.

Several concrete barriers had been stacked off to one side. Max and Sandra slipped behind before peeking at the ceremony. Upon his first look, Max knew this was going to be more dangerous than the previous gatherings.

As before, the cloaked figures formed a circle. However, this was not just any circle. A pentagram had been marked in the dirt with white chalk. At each of the five star points, a single candle had been placed. Each candle was a different color — red, blue, white, yellow, and black. The flickering light reflected off the concrete pillars and walls under the bridge. In the surrounding dark, the dim candlelight made the space feel enclosed and tight like a dungeon passage.

Using three equidistant points on the pentagram, a triangle had been drawn with yellow chalk. At two of the triangle points, they had placed symbols to represent the past tragedies. The one on the left had a small stool, and sitting on the stool, Max could see a rusted, slave collar — a symbol of all those buried at Odd Fellows Cemetery. From a distance, the collar looked to be authentic.

Another stool on the second point of the triangle had an old hunting rifle. Max recalled that Charlie Lawson had used several weapons to massacre his family including a rifle. Over the years, that particular weapon disappeared. Could that really be the same gun?

At the final point of the triangle — which matched the top point of the pentagram — Isaac Brown stood with PB at his side.

Max's heart leapt to his throat. He wanted to sprint under that bridge, kick those candles away, grab PB in the confusion, and escape. Of course, that would fail. He would never get close to PB. This had to be done carefully. Thoughtfully.

"Remember," he said to Sandra, "we have to get PB first. Once he's safe, we can worry about stopping the spell."

Keeping his eyes on the ceremony, Drummond said, "Say the word and I'll go freeze them all. It'll hurt something awful, but I'll do it."

Sandra shook her head. "They will definitely be warded against ghosts. Probably witches, too. This is the culmination of decades of work. Madame Yan is not going to leave any of it open for you to swoop in and save the day."

The Soro Group started on a melodic chant. Isaac lifted his hands and spoke but Max could not decipher the words.

"We have to get closer," he said.

Sandra said, "If we go out there, we'll get spotted."

Pointing to a large mobile generator parked just in front of the bridge, Drummond said, "Get ready to run for that."

He swept forward, rose up into the air, and passed over the bridge. His pale figure descended on the opposite side. He studied the ground until he found a short piece of discarded metal. With a hearty yell, Drummond lifted the small metal bar a few inches off the ground and dropped it. As he danced around waving his burning hands, the metal bar clattered on the ground — and the entire Soro Group looked to the far end where the noise had come from.

Max and Sandra bolted across in the open. They stayed upright, moving as fast as possible, while everybody's attention was turned away. Sliding in behind the generator, Max could only hear his heavy breathing. With Sandra's arm on his shoulder, he calmed and listened closely — until he heard Isaac without trouble.

Jerking his head, Isaac sent one of his followers to investigate the noise. Max and Sandra held still. Max even held his breath. When the follower returned with a shrug, Isaac continued.

But the chanting had ceased, and Max could tell by the way Isaac comported himself that this time, things were going to be different. This time, the groundwork had been laid and the bulk of the spell now needed to be cast.

As if to erase any doubt, Isaac spouted off a flurry of ancient words and all the candle flames lifted high in the air. When they settled back to normal, the cloaked figures lowered to their knees without a sound. They were scared.

Max could easily imagine that many of them only half-believed in the promises of the Soro Group. But now, Isaac Brown was proving himself. This night, this gathering, had suddenly become darkly real to them all.

"Tonight is a special night," Isaac said. "Tonight, after almost a decade, my son, my flesh and blood, stands here with me. Tonight, he will learn the truth of his legacy, and through it, we will fulfill the promise I have made to all of you."

With robotic motions, one of the followers rose and stepped up toward PB. This figure carried a heavy looking vest — almost a flak jacket.

Isaac continued, "Those of you who have been with me long enough know that this bit of magic we wield is very dangerous. Members in our past have died in their attempt to turn fortune their way. But some of us have had success, too. That is how we know it is worth the risk. As with all things in life, the higher the risk, the higher the reward. And what could be more risky than your life? So you know the reward is equally great."

Isaac took the vest from the follower and held it above his head. Max did not like this. He could not say what was off exactly, but the whole thing seemed fishy.

"Is that part of the spell?" he asked.

Sandra frowned. "If it is, Madame Yan kept it well-hidden."

Drummond descended behind them. "You were right. They have all kinds of wards running in there. I'm guessing each one is carved into those candles. Strong stuff. I could feel it even as I flew overhead."

Sandra said, "Maybe it's just a group thing. Like a Rotary club vest."

"Then why haven't we seen them before?" Max asked.

As Isaac helped PB put on the vest, he made sure to keep eye contact with the boy. It zipped up the front and a strange layer of cloth flapped over to secure it on the opposite side. Isaac fished out PB's necklace so that it rested in the open on the boy's chest. Beaming, Isaac pulled his own necklace out from beneath his shirt. It had a matching pendant.

Isaac Brown placed an object like an oversized pen in PB's hand and whispered in the boy's ear. Max saw it register on PB's face right away. The surprise followed by the horror. PB stared at this pen in his hand and his arm shook.

Max's stomach hit the floor. "Oh, no."

Raising his voice, Isaac Brown said, "In each of our steps toward tonight, we have been required to shed blood. Ideally, those sacrifices would have been given freely. And in some ways they were. But tonight — tonight no hand may touch the sacrifice. No soul can assist. Our ceremony can only benefit one individual, so the sacrifice must be related through blood to that individual. Thus, tonight the sacrifice is my son. He stands before us to benefit me." He turned to PB. "Sorry, son. You are holding what is called a dead man's trigger. As long as you hold it tight, you will live. But when you let it go, the vest will explode."

PB's eyes shimmered. He started to move, perhaps make a run for it, but the follower standing behind him clamped down on his shoulders.

"Careful. You should put your focus on that trigger." As he spoke, the rest of the cloaked followers backed away several feet, still maintaining a circle. PB was guided into the center of the pentagram. Isaac continued, "I'm sure you had the thought of letting go in an attempt to kill us all. Take us with you. That won't work. This is not a terrorist's vest intended to cause as much destruction as possible. The explosives here are small and directed so that most of the blast will go inward. At this distance from you, we will all be quite safe."

"Not safe from me," Max said as he stepped away from the generator and rushed straight in.

Chapter 29

WITH A CARTOONISH SNEER, Isaac Brown said, "I can't say I'm surprised. Heck, I would've been disappointed if you hadn't shown."

Max clenched his fists as he stormed forward. Isaac snapped a finger at one of his followers, and the cloaked figure broke away from the circle to intercept. Rolling his head, Max raised his fists. He expected no less.

The figure flipped back the hood and revealed a thick-necked, flat-nosed bruiser of a man. The way he thumped toward Max with all the grace of a clumsy giant, Max thought the man did not have much fighting experience. At least, not good fighting. He probably relied on his bulk to end conflicts with only a couple of punches.

But Max had continued his Tae Kwon Do training and knew how to move. When the big fellow stepped in and hauled off a haymaker, it was over. For the big guy.

Max ducked the punch, stayed low, and thrust his palm right into the man's solar plexus. Twisting at the waist as he delivered the blow, Max sent all of his force into that one small section of the chest like a metal piston blasting forth.

The big guy crashed to his knees, gasping for breath, clutching his chest. Max straightened and walked on, his eyes zeroing in on Isaac.

"Well, well," Isaac said, still cocky, still confident. "Looks like we have a fighter." Another flick of his finger sent another one of his followers.

This time when the hood fell back, Max discovered a hard-looking woman. Real barfly type. If either she or Isaac thought Max would not hit a woman, then they seriously misread the situation. Because nothing would stop him from getting PB back.

The woman, however, did have a few surprises. She began her attack further away than he expected, running forward and growling like a rabid dog. He set his foot back in a fighting stance, watched her approach, and wondered why she would telegraph her attack with such blatant abandon. Turned out, at the last moment, she dove forward, somersaulted, and popped up with a low punch aiming for the groin.

Muscle memory saved Max. Before he could consciously act, his body moved. He blocked, shoving her fist off course and into his thigh. A dull throb raced up his leg, promising a thick cloud of purple and black bruising to be with him for at least a week.

For a half-second, the woman stared at Max and Max stared back. Then he clocked her in the jaw. Before she could reset her legs, he kicked at the side of the nearest knee. It bent at a funny angle and she screamed as she went down.

Max resumed his steady stride. Seeing the doubt ripple across Isaac's brow, Max allowed himself one arrogant breath — all of that martial arts training had finally paid off big. But then Isaac flicked his hand twice, and two burly men removed their hoods.

The one on the left looked to be middle-aged, probably a banker or a lawyer, but he held himself in a balanced stance with tight fists — he had some training, too. The man on the right was young, pushing thirty, and if he lacked anything in skill, he would make up for it with youthful energy.

Max settled once again into a fighting stance, once again raised his fists, once again readied for a fight. But in the back of his mind, he knew that taking on more than one person at a time went beyond any of his training. He would do his best, but he only had a few tricks up his sleeve.

"It's not looking too good," Isaac said. "If it will help you give up sooner, I can throw in a third person. Or maybe I'll join."

"I think I can help," Sandra said as she stepped out from

behind the generator. With her hands splayed open, a red ball of energy formed. It glowed beneath her face casting stark shadows up into her hair.

All of the Soro Group — those revealed and those still hiding beneath their hoods — stepped back.

Isaac glowered. "Don't be cowards. She's one lady putting on a light show. We have the power of true magic with us."

Sandra could not hold back her mocking laugh. To Max, she said, "Duck."

Max dropped to the dirt as Sandra unleashed the energy she had gathered. It spread out like a crimson fan, expanding the further it traveled. Slapping into the members of the Soro Group, the energy lifted them into the air and threw them back several feet. Max knew the blast had not been intended to harm anybody, certainly not to kill anybody, but part of him wished she had been willing to do more damage.

Helping Max back to his feet, she took his hand and pulled him in a rush to get to PB. The boy sat in the center of the circle with his back to them. His head hung low.

"Are you hurt?" Max had missed if the energy blast went over PB's head or not.

"It's us, sweetie," Sandra said. "We're here to take you home."

She put her hand on PB's back, but he shucked it off. "Go away," he said.

Max stepped around and knelt in front of PB. "Don't worry. We're going to figure out how to get you out of this safely."

Lifting his tear-stained face, PB said, "Leave me alone. Go back to J. He's worth saving."

"Don't say that. You're worth every bit as much to us as J."

"I rejected you. I did the stupid thing. I always do the stupid thing. I deserve to be sitting here like this."

"No," Max said. The word sounded weak to his ears but not because he agreed with PB — he clearly didn't — but because he had no idea how to respond.

"Max!"

Looking up, Max saw a startled expression on Sandra's face.

He knew without doubt that one of the Soro Group would be attacking him from behind. He knew this because he saw the barfly coming up behind Sandra.

The blow to his head sent the world spinning. He saw the faces of the Soro Group whipping by. He saw the construction equipment in the distance. He saw the hollow look in PB's eyes. Worst of all — he saw PB's hand shaking as the boy tried to keep a tight grip on a dead man's trigger.

Chapter 30

ALTHOUGH MAX AND SANDRA NEVER BLACKED OUT, they were dazed enough to be easily controlled. By the time Max's head began to clear, he and Sandra had been tied back-to-back and thrown into the center of the circle. PB stayed at their side, unwilling to look at either of them. He sat on the ground, stared at the trigger in his hand, and shuddered.

Up to this point, Max's attention had been so focused on rescuing PB, he had taken little notice of basic matters — like the heat. But now, under this bridge with his body tied, he became exceedingly aware of the sweat streaming from his brow, of the salty taste in his mouth as it slipped between his lips, of the burn from coarse rope rubbing against his slick wrists. If they didn't die from blowing up next to PB, Max thought they had a good chance of dying from dehydration.

The Soro Group huddled several feet away. Isaac Brown stood off by himself. At length, he walked back and motioned for the group to return. They filed in to form a large circle around their victims. Max smirked. It was hot enough for him — those poor bastards had to wear heavy cloaks.

Isaac Brown paused to gather the full attention of his followers. "I know some of you might be troubled by what you've seen, but we cannot stop now. We have come right up to the end. The things we seek stand before us, waiting to be taken. I know some of you look at these two people and think *No, that's too much.*"

"I'm one of them," Max said. Anything to distract them, stall them, buy every possible second he could. He had no plan, but experience had taught him that extra time often made all the difference.

"My friends," Isaac continued with a warming gesture. "I understand that this woman's display may have caused you to second-guess yourselves. But I implore you — take control of your way of thinking."

"You should second-guess yourselves," Max went on. "This man is a liar and you're all being fooled." He knew the odds of changing the mind of a cult follower were slim, but better to throw all his ideas out than regret holding back. If he could get even one person to slow the proceedings by asking a question or two, then it would be worthwhile.

But Isaac knew his audience well. "The fact that this woman, this insignificant and powerless fool, was able to use magic is proof that magic exists. It is proof that we have the power right here, right in our grasp, to fulfill all my years of study and training. All that you have done will provide wealth for each of us in time. When my riches rain down upon me, you will know that the sacrifices you have been called upon to make will be worth it. You will know that fortune awaits you."

To Sandra, Max whispered, "What can we do? How do we stop this spell?"

"If we weren't stuck together, I'd say we should do what always works — break the circle, kick down the candles. Anything like that."

"That'll do it?"

"Sometimes. Sometimes not. It depends on the spell. Madame Yan created this to be a tough one. I'm not making any promises."

Max looked to PB. Perhaps he could encourage the boy to disrupt the spell. But PB's entire brain focused on keeping that vest from exploding. From what Max could see, PB had not even heard anything being said. He had shut down into his own world. It was completely understandable, but not very helpful.

Like a magician, Isaac pulled a piece of paper from his sleeve. He unfolded the paper and read the phonetic spellings of the archaic words. Those of his group who were not frightened before, no doubt became nervous right away. The moment he started his recitation, the air shifted.

Max felt the hairs on his arms rise as if a cold front had moved in. His mouth dried, and he heard a ringing in his ears, too. Should he start smelling burnt toast, he would fear a stroke. But he knew exactly what was happening.

With frustrated impatience, Sandra groaned. "Don't do this. You'll regret it. You really think a witch will play fair?"

Isaac nodded to Big Guy. The man clumped forward toward the red candle. Licking his fingers, he bent over and snuffed out the flame. As the smoke trailed into the air like a gray snake dancing towards the sky, Big Guy rejoined the circle.

Sandra said, "Madame Yan is using you."

"Of course she's using me," Isaac said, his face flushed at the interruption. "You really think after all these years I would simply walk into something like this without learning about it? Do you really think I would have gone through all the trouble, all the sacrifice, all the pains I have endured and simply accept a witch at her word? But she's made a mistake — her arrogance blinds her to the fact that I'm the one using her."

With another motion of his head, Isaac sent the banker forward to snuff out the blue candle.

Leaning closer to PB, Max said, "I know it's hard right now. I know everything is a confusing mess. I know it's even difficult to believe what's real and what isn't, who's lying to you and who's telling the truth, all of it. But I promise you this — life is worth pushing through. Don't give up. You keep holding that trigger. You hold it as long as you can. We're working to find some way out of this."

He hoped he told the truth. It all came down to flipping the order of his intended plan. Instead of saving PB and then destroying the spell, it appeared they had to do it the other way around. Once the spell was destroyed, they would be able to break free of this group and do what they could to save PB.

At least, Sandra had played upon Isaac's ego. He had stopped reciting the spell while he made sure everybody knew how brilliant he was in orchestrating this moment. He went on, "That wretched, filthy hag thinks she is smarter than me? She really thinks she's pulling one over on me? It's ridiculous. The

Soro Group has been working with her kind for generations. We're not novices. We're not little wide-eyed, gullible fools who are amazed by the awesome power of a witch. Not one bit. In fact, we are so much smarter than any witch. After all, the witches sold their souls to gain all their power. We merely use them. We remain intact."

Max felt Sandra's hands rubbing against his wrists. A noble effort, but he did not think they had enough time to cut through the ropes. She said, "A witch as smart as Madame Yan knows full well what you're trying to do. I have no doubt she's accounted for it."

Isaac read more of the spell and indicated for Barfly to snuff out the white candle. "Let me tell you something about Madame Yan. She hides out underground thinking she is some master puppeteer controlling all of us. She thinks that this spell will grant her untold power and make whatever I want pointless. But that's because she thinks so low of man. She thinks all I want is money. She thinks all men only want money or power or sex."

"Isn't that true?"

"I feel bad for your husband if you think that way. Men don't care about those things. Not real men." Isaac had the young man snuff out the yellow candle. "Money, power, sex — those are the goals of a politician. But for a real man they are merely tools. Are you listening, PB? Your father is dispensing some good advice. From the dawn of time, real men used whatever tools were available to reshape the world however he saw fit. To make the world better for his people to live in. This group here — these are my people. And I will use the money and power this spell provides to reshape Winston-Salem and perhaps all of North Carolina so that we few here will have a better world."

Isaac spouted out the final words of the spell. With a swagger, he sauntered up to the black candle bent over and pinched out the flame. Backing to his original position, he laughed like a giddy child waiting to open his birthday presents.

In a blinding flash, all five candles reignited with sharp green firelight. Their unnatural glow reflected around the pentagram and trailed off like a sickness in the air.

Max's thigh heated up. At first, he thought it was a reaction to this next stage of the spell. However, as the heat continued to press on one small part of his leg, he had a different idea — Leroy's little book. While Isaac blabbed on about how powerful and superior he would soon be, Max glanced out toward the generator and construction vehicles. Drummond stood there, anxious to enter.

With him, Max saw four other ghosts.

One wore a military outfit and had the tough build to go with it. One was a young man with a panther's glint in his eyes. One woman wore chainmail from head to foot and held a huge sword. And one woman had to be Miss 1800s.

"Be ready," Max whispered.

Sandra looked up. "Drummond brought friends."

"I know. The fact that I can see them means Leroy's book in my pocket is working again."

"Are you controlling it? Can you tell it what to do?"

"One hundred percent, absolutely not. Just be ready for something to happen."

The book continued to grow hotter. Not painful yet, but he worried it might get that way. Though he had no desire to suffer third-degree burns, Max decided that disfiguring his leg would be far better than dying at the hands of a lowly cult leader like Isaac Brown.

Leaning his head back so that it pressed against Sandra, Max said, "Chicks still dig scars, right?"

Isaac Brown brought his hands together, clasping them over the green tinted smoke rising from the black candle. His prattling had crescendoed to the point that his voice echoed off the walls, loud and strong. "It is here, my friends. I can feel the power growing around us. This spell, this time, will work. We will have the money. We will have the power. We will control all the magic. We will control all the witches."

The green flames rose, washing every face with its distorting hues. Max smelled burning. He glanced down and saw the pocket of his pant leg smoldering.

"Whatever's about to happen," he said, nudging PB with his shoulder, "whatever you hear or see, you hold on to that trigger. Help is about to come."

The charred remains of his pocket fell to the side and smoke rose from the book on his leg.

"Hey, Isaac." Max projected his voice so that it stood above all other sounds. "You forget about the ghosts."

Isaac frowned. "Ghosts?"

From the burning against his leg, Max knew the time had arrived. "Drummond, come on in."

The candle flames shot up ten feet. They burned as bright as the nighttime worklamps lining the entire construction site. They burned hot — so hot that the candles rapidly melted into colorful puddles of wax. And in doing so, they melted off the wards carved into each colorful candle.

Drummond and his ghostly friends rushed in.

Chapter 31

THE INSTANT THE WARDS WENT DOWN, Drummond's four ghost friends swept in hungry for a fight. Panther Eyes shot forth as if he had waited centuries for this moment. Enduring the pain of touching the corporeal world, he grabbed the banker by the neck while kicking Big Guy in the knee. Grunts and yelps flavored the air with a haphazard rhythm.

Military Man worked his way through several still-cloaked figures while the Swordswoman chose to slice across her path, freezing every living thing she touched. And Miss 1800s — she smacked Barfly across the face with an open hand.

"What's happening?" PB said, his voice shaking as members of the Soro Group convulsed and spasmed for no apparent reason.

"What have you done?" The words stretched and warped like the ghost that uttered them. Pulling up from the ground, Wilson Klein emerged — straining against his tether to the cemetery. His face distorted as his cursed soul fought the return to his murder site.

"You'll all pay." Another whispery, wet voice called — Jackson Wheeler, his ghost throat sliced open like the day he died, grabbed at those who had betrayed him.

But neither Wheeler nor Klein stayed for long. Their tethers were too new, too strong. As they snapped away, Isaac hustled into the circle and hauled PB to his feet. "Come with me, son. Your fake parents have ruined our chance at happiness tonight." PB stumbled at his father's side as they hastened west toward the Marshall Street Bridge.

"Don't," Max said, straining against his ropes. But PB never looked back.

As the ghosts continued their attack, they began to fade from Max's view. Glancing down at his leg, he saw the page from Leroy's book — nothing more than ashes.

Drummond flew in fast. "I thought you two would never get around to dropping that ward." Wincing at the pain, he worked to untie Sandra.

Sandra said, "I'm just grateful you brought help."

"More help than you realize — that G.I. is an expert with bombs. Once we finish up here, we can help PB."

"Fantastic," Max said, turning to let PB know. But PB wasn't there.

Freed, Sandra pulled away. To Drummond, she said, "Follow Isaac. I'll take care of Max."

Drummond soared off as Sandra went to work on Max's ropes. "It's going to be okay. It's going to be okay," she murmured like a mantra. "I can be a good witch. I can be a good witch."

A crack formed in Max's heart. Over the last three days, he had heard Sandra's doubts and fears, but he had been so wrapped up with his own concerns about being a good father that he never let her side of things sink in. Once freed, he whirled around and pulled her into his arms. "You are a good witch and a great mother. Don't ever think otherwise. Now, let's go get our boy."

Lacing their fingers together, they walked away from the jerking bodies of the Soro Group. Max grinned — only seeing Drummond seemed just fine. He preferred to avoid the horror of other ghosts from now on. Several of the Soro Group lay unconscious on the ground. A few attempted to throw wild punches in the air. They never had a chance.

"Thank you," Sandra said, nodding at a handful of empty spaces. To Max, she added, "They're leaving now."

Limping as they walked — the burn on his leg sent waves of fiery pain through his body every time he put too much weight on it — Max squinted ahead. Drummond waved for them to hurry over.

"Go, go," Max said, urging Sandra onward. He quickened

his pace, hobbling out from under the Cherry Street Bridge. Drummond hovered over Isaac and PB like a beacon. Max wondered why the ghost did not simply give Isaac a little bit of brain freeze, but then he recalled the pendant around Isaac's neck — the one that matched PB's. Any gambler would be willing to place money down that Madame Yan had given Isaac his own personal ghost ward.

Sandra dashed under the Marshall Street Bridge and kept going. As Max followed, he spotted Isaac and PB scrambling up the dirt incline. Sandra rushed to catch up.

Off to his right, Max spied a long cable running from the city street all the way down into the construction area. Picking it up, he discovered that it was heavy but manageable. With the help of this improvised rope, Max pulled up the incline quicker than he could have on his own.

When he reached the top, he did his best approximation of running to reach the others. As Sandra stepped onto the level surface, Max was there to lend a hand. He pulled her up and they hurried on together.

Scanning ahead, and with the help of Drummond's pale light, Max spotted Isaac and PB — and Max's body froze inside.

Isaac should have taken PB to the right, crossing by some homes, and into the city, to be lost amongst the people and cars and winding streets. But as he stepped in that direction, two police cars sped by with lights flashing and sirens crying out. They headed back toward the Cherry Street Bridge. When Leroy's book destroyed the wards against the ghosts, the wards hiding the Soro Group's activities also went away. Somebody living nearby finally noticed.

Reacting to the police more than thinking logically, Isaac turned left — probably expecting to cross the bridge over the construction site and keep going away from the city. But the Spruce Street Bridge had been demolished as part of the restructuring of traffic flow. The bridge ended with ragged concrete and rebar while bits of pipes and wiring poked out in a haphazard manner.

By the time Max and Sandra reached the start of the bridge, Isaac held PB only twenty feet away — backed up against the edge. One step further and both of them would plummet to their deaths.

"Sorry," Drummond said. "I can't get any closer to them. I tried — but he's warded."

"We know," Sandra said.

"You don't know anything," Isaac said, shifting PB in front of him, holding the boy tight with one arm.

Drummond said, "It's not just that. When I tried to stop them, the ward blasted out energy to push me back — that energy has cracked this end of the bridge. It won't take much to fall apart beneath them."

Max put out his hand to PB. "Don't do this."

Isaac's face twisted up tight. "He's my boy. You don't get to steal him from me."

"Nobody has to die. But if you're determined — at least let PB make his own choice."

With a twitch of his cheek, Isaac pushed PB aside. Max heard bits of concrete break off. His heart dropped as they smashed on the ground far below.

"They'll never trust you," Isaac said to his son. "You'll never be anything more than the boy that rejected them. Every time they put food on the table for you to eat, every time they buy you clothes to keep you warm or pay their mortgage so that you have a roof over your head or do anything for you, in the backs of their minds they'll be thinking that you rejected them. That you'll do it again." Isaac put out his hand. "But you come with me, and we can build something real. I'm here for you. I'm the one who will never doubt your loyalty."

Sandra said, "If PB goes with you, he's going to die."

"I've seen magic." Isaac stomped away a few steps, loosening more concrete. "I've glimpsed the power that is out there. And it can be stronger than death."

PB frowned. "Is that why you were willing to put this vest on me?"

The malicious grin on Isaac's face made Max want to throw

up. "Of course, my son. You don't think I'd ever want to hurt you, do you? And kill you? Never. But I needed my followers to believe that the sacrifice was real. I'm sorry if it scared you. But everything I've said is true — I've seen that magic is real. When we get out of here, I will take that vest off you because we don't need it anymore. We'll find some other spell to get our fortune. Don't you worry, though. You would never have been dead for long. I would have brought you back."

Max took one step closer. "Don't listen to him, PB. He's desperate. He'll say anything. I mean, come on — magic?"

PB's feet danced an inch towards Isaac and an inch towards Max. As crazy as the situation seemed, Max understood PB's behavior. If Isaac told the truth — and PB wanted it to be the truth — then the vest never mattered. It was a falsehood designed to fool others. But if Max told the truth, then his life was in grave danger.

Isaac must have read the situation, too. "Look at me, son. I'm your father." He lifted his pendant, and PB focused on the symbol. The boy's free hand brushed the matching pendant on his chest.

Max pointed as if he had caught a magician attempting sleight of hand. "The pendant. He's manipulating you with the pendant."

Isaac's eye glinted. "Just a little magic to ease your suffering. I know how hard all of this has been on you. As your loving father, I want to make life better, easier for you. If you think about it, this pendant is your proof of all I have said. Magic is real, and I know how to use it. If I did not know the things I said to be true, why would I have brought us over here? Why would I have risked our lives? Why would I have gone through any of this trouble?"

"That's right," Sandra said. "Think about it. Why did this man really go to all this trouble?"

PB turned his questioning eyes upon Isaac. Max caught it — just a flash, but it stabbed out like a searchlight in the night. Max stepped ahead once more. Thrusting his hand out, he said, "PB, push on through."

Isaac lunged forward, clasping PB's arm. "No. You belong to me."

PB shoved back, and a large crack cut across the roadway. Max's eyes widened as he saw the edge of the demolished bridge crumbling beneath Isaac and PB's feet.

As Isaac screamed and tumbled into the darkness below, Max jumped forward, grabbing for any part of PB he could. But his fingers only brushed the side of PB's arm. In that same second, Drummond dove at them, letting the ward hit him hard. As he bounced off the ward's field, he willed himself solid for a fleeting moment — long enough to bang into PB and knock the boy into Max's arms. Max clutched the boy close while ripping the gold necklace and pendant loose.

Isaac's screams had ceased. Only the crying of PB and Max and Sandra could be heard.

Chapter 32

THEY HAD ONLY A SHORT TIME FOR TEARS. Wiping his eyes, Max settled on his knees with PB doing the same in front of him. Sandra stepped behind, supposedly to offer a comforting hand on the back of PB's head while she looked up how to disarm a bomb on her phone, but in truth, they simply did not want PB seeing her talk to the empty air. Drummond had gone to fetch his military friend, the bomb expert, and until he arrived, they needed to calm down.

"It's going to be fine," Sandra said. "Don't worry about anything that's happened until now. You weren't yourself, and you have nothing to feel bad about."

Max put his hand over PB's to help control the trigger. "You've done an incredible job up to this point. Don't give up. Only a little longer to go."

PB's tears flowed free as his body continually shivered. "I don't understand any of this. I could see everything happening but my brain got all foggy. He said it was magic."

"What do you think?"

"That pendant — could it have been coated with something? Drugs of some kind?"

"Something like that. I think so. Your father was a bad man and —"

"He wasn't my father. You're my father."

Max said nothing — he could not get his throat to open. His chest, his heart, his entire being tightened into a ball that simply wanted to envelop PB and hold the boy forever. He managed a nod and what he hoped looked like an expression of thanks.

"Okay," Drummond said as he flew up from the construction site. "This is Roy. He served two tours in

Vietnam, and he knows a thing or two about explosives."

Max watched as Sandra focused on the air to her right. She then looked back at Max. "I've got what we need. This won't be too bad. You both listen to me, and follow my instructions exactly, and we'll survive this. First thing we need to do is follow a few wires."

As Sandra detailed each step, Max and PB obeyed. During the breaks when she received more information from Roy, Max talked to PB — to keep the boy's mind off of the horror of the moment. To keep his own mind off it, too. "I suppose you have a lot of questions about the things you saw tonight."

PB shrugged. "My head was a mess for most of it. But it's not that hard to figure out. I mean, what do you expect from a bunch of cultist nutjobs? My father — I mean, Isaac — he ran a huge cult racket, and when he couldn't get me to join, he drugged me. Right?"

"I guess so."

Sandra's shoulders relaxed. "Almost there. Looks like things are going to be easier." She gave the next few commands which required Max to swipe a few tools from the construction site. When he returned, he carefully snipped two wires and then started cutting at the top of the covering locked over the zipper. As he worked, he said, "I just want you to know that it's okay if you still care about your dad."

"Why would I do that? He tried to kill me."

"I know. But family is a weird thing. Sometimes we find ourselves caring about the people who hurt us. Especially when they're our parents."

PB placed his hand on top of Max to stop him for a moment. Once he had Max's full attention, he said, "I know who my parents are. I know what family is. Blood is not family. People think it is, but that's an illusion. It's an excuse people use to avoid fighting for the real thing. But if anything, this night has proven that we are family."

The corner of Max's mouth rose. "My mother has really been teaching you well."

Max finished cutting away the last of the security covering.

Roy suspected that Isaac had little knowledge of building explosive vests and that proved to be true. Once access to the zipper had been achieved, they carefully unfastened the vest and removed it. Sandra wasted no time tossing it over the edge of the bridge, and PB gratefully let go of the trigger. They heard a distinctive pop and stared at each other.

Fearing he might pass out, Max put his arms around his wife and son. "Come on. Let's go home."

Chapter 33

MAX STOOD AT HIS BEDROOM CLOSET and stared at the clothes hanging from the rod. Five days had gone by. For a day or two, the media outlets jumped all over the story of an apparent group suicide performed by a bizarre cult. The police happily let that narrative takeover — partially because some in the department knew the truth and had been ordered to silence matters, partially because some in the department were terrified of any other possible truth.

Sandra and J appeared to be handling their return to normal life fairly well. On the other hand, PB had suffered a truly traumatic experience, and while he put on a brave face, Max saw the way PB turned sullen and distant when he thought he was alone. But Max recognized those moments because he suffered from them, too. So, he did the smart thing. He told Sandra and immediately set up appointments with a psychologist. Despite Sandra's version of a brave face, Max watched her closely — just in case.

He reached into the closet for a shirt and stopped. It was the same yellow shirt he wore when Cecily Hull had sent a police officer to the house late at night, when Max first encountered the Odd Fellows Cemetery, when everything had begun. It still had the wine stain. There had been no time yet to get it cleaned. A few days ago, when he visited Cecily Hull again, he wore that yellow shirt and grinned inwardly when she curled her lip at the sight of its rumpled glory.

He provided a full report, holding back nothing, and she surprised him on several levels. She appeared to have true concern over PB's well-being, and she also displayed genuine remorse over the death of Isaac Brown. She even tossed in a bonus to Max's fee.

Most of all, she expressed gratitude that when given the choice of who should attempt to control magic in North Carolina, Max had chosen her. "After all," Cecily said, "you could quite easily have chosen Madame Yan. You could have let her scheme with the Soro Group succeed and perhaps you could even have gained a position of power under her."

"I prefer the devil I know."

"I'm hardly a devil. I can't really even cast a spell."

"Maybe not, but you managed to use me and my son to get rid of some of your competition. The Soro Group is destroyed and Madame Yan's spell that took decades to perfect failed. Anybody else thinking about taking you on will think twice. Unless Madame Yan has a backup plan."

"Oh, I don't think we'll have to worry about her."

Max shook his head. "All of this just to continue the same crap your family has always done."

"I should think after all this time, you would have learned that having somebody in charge is necessary. I've told you that I do not intend to govern magic the way my family has done in the past. They used their power to control people and enrich themselves. Much like a politician. But I have a greater vision, one that will bring peace and prosperity to all."

"You sure sound like a politician."

Contorting her mouth into an awkward smile, Cecily poured two tumblers of brandy and offered a toast. "To the Hull Organization. Though you fail to see it, we will have a wonderful future ahead of us."

While it turned his stomach, Max raised his glass and drank. Better than kissing her ring again.

The following day, he and Sandra drove out to Lexington for a visit with Madame Yan. When they arrived, however, they found the house abandoned. Madame Yan and Cheryl-Lynn had packed up everything and left. They must have paid a lot of money to have a moving company arrive on such short notice.

The rooms were bare — furniture gone, clothes gone, dishes and glasses gone, even the curtains and curtain rods had vanished. Max went all the way underground to Madame Yan's private apartment. Empty. Her cluttered rooms had been gutted. The air smelled stale as if the place had been unoccupied for many years. Only a few wood shelves and a few unused boxes remained. Not a lipstick in sight.

Staring at the empty apartment, Max could only hope they never saw either woman again. He doubted he would be so lucky.

The Sandwich Boys burst into laughter from down the hall. That brought a smile to Max's lips. Sandra entered the bedroom and popped a suitcase onto the bed.

Leaning her head back toward the door, she said, "Boys, get packing already."

"Yes, Sandra," they said in singsong unison.

Coming up behind Max, she put her arms around his waist. With her chin snuggling his shoulder blade, she said, "I think this is a good idea."

He chuckled. "Of course you do. You've been wanting to go to the beach for a long time." He turned around in her arms. "But I think it's a good thing, too. We need to get away. A little vacation."

J knocked on the door as he walked in. "Hey, I was wondering if Uncle Marshall is going to be coming with us."

Before Max could answer, Drummond flew through the outside wall. "You bet I'm coming," he said. "I couldn't let my favorite nephew down."

J shared a conspiratorial nod with the ghost before running off. Max turned to his partner. "What kind of trouble are you planning with that boy?"

"Just some wholesome good times at a beach. Y'know, a little bonding time. Besides, it's my duty as his uncle to teach him all the important things."

"Do I even want to know what those things are?"

"Probably not. Think of it like the education you can't provide because you have to be a good parent."

Max gazed at Sandra but she laughed. "Don't look at me. You're the one who brought this ghost into our lives."

With a flick of his hat, Drummond said, "Best decision he ever made."

Max turned back to his closet. He grabbed the yellow shirt, rolled it into a ball, and tossed it in the trash. "Now I'm ready to pack."

Sandra said, "Okay. No backing out. We're going to the beach."

"That's right. We're going to the beach." He leaned over and kissed her. "As a family."

Afterword

Thank you, once again, for riding along with me, Max, Sandra, Drummond, and all the rest of the gang. This series will forever hold a special place in my heart, and from the comments you all send me, the same can be said for you. But before I offend Drummond by getting too mushy, let's get into what you really want out of this Afterword:

Of the history involved in this tale, the biggest event was the Lawson Family Massacre. Everything I wrote about it is entirely true. I took no liberties with this horrible event other than in describing the current state of the location. Since it is private property, I decided not to act like Max and trespass. I did, however, use available images from Google Maps to get a rough idea of the area. If you're interested in learning about the Lawson family and finding out in great detail about everything that led up to the murders, the murders themselves, and the aftermath, then you should check out *The Meaning of our Tears* by Trudy J. Smith. This well-researched book relies heavily on firsthand accounts which give the book an authenticity and depth you won't find anywhere else.

Odd Fellows Cemetery is real as is the sad circumstances of its existence. The construction of Business 40 is real and ongoing as of this writing, though the tragedies surrounding it are mostly from my imagination. However, the history of the road is true, including the controversy over the Hawthorne Curve. Oh, and Lexington BBQ is a real and wonderful place to eat. If you're ever in the area and want to try what the real thing tastes like, you can do no better.

Tragedy groups, to the best of my knowledge, do not exist. I made them up for the story. Though, I admit, I would not be surprised to discover some version of the idea either once did or currently does exist. After all the years writing this series and all the research I have done, I don't shock easily.

I'd like to use this last bit of space to thank Dr. Darin Kennedy for his friendship and his medical knowledge, Francesca Resta for another incredible cover, my Launch Team for their vigilant eye and joyous encouragement, and of course, to my wife and son for their constant support.

Most of all, I can never stop thanking you, my readers. None of these stories get to exist without you reading them. Thank you.

About the Author

Stuart Jaffe is the madman behind *The Max Porter Paranormal Mysteries,* the *Nathan K* thrillers, *The Parallel Society* series, *The Malja Chronicles, The Bluesman, Founders, Real Magic,* and so much more. His unique brand of old pulp adventure mixed with a contemporary sensibility brings out the best in a variety of SF/F sub-genres. He trained in martial arts for over a decade until a knee injury ended that practice. Now, he plays lead guitar in a local blues band, *The Bootleggers,* and enjoys life on a small farm in rural North Carolina. For those who continue to keep count, the animal list is as follows: one dog, two cats, two aquatic turtles, and fifteen chickens. The horse is now at a new pasture. She's having a wonderful time hanging with a herd of thirty other horses. Much better for her. As best as he's been able to manage, Stuart has made sure that the chickens do not live in the house.

.

www.ingramcontent.com/pod-product-compliance
Lightning Source LLC
Chambersburg PA
CBHW030530310726
48979CB00010B/1868/J

* 9 7 8 1 9 6 3 5 1 7 0 5 7 *